What I think about most is cruising Main Street in a Ford pickup truck, an F-250 four-wheel drive with a stick shift. Also I think about girls— town girls to take home after school, town girls to ride next to me in the cab of my pickup, or in the back, or leaning on the roll bar. Beautiful town girls with blond hair bouncing on their shoulders, with names like Jinny, Amber, and Blythe. Names that whisper of love.

I was hoping to have a chance with one of them this year, but so far I have been followed around by three scared and skinny Dudettes with names only a Bear Flats mother would name a daughter: Mona, Netty, and Helen.

Here at the Scenic-Vu Motel

Thelma Hatch Wyss
AR B.L.: 4.4
Points: 4.0

Thelma Hatch Wyss

HERE AT THE
Scenic-Vu
Motel

A HarperKeypoint Book

An Imprint of HarperCollins*Publishers*

This book was made possible, in part, by a grant cosponsored by Judy Blume and the Society of Children's Book Writers.

Here at the Scenic-Vu Motel
Copyright © 1988 by Thelma Hatch Wyss
Typography by Joyce Hopkins

Library of Congress Cataloging-in-Publication Data
Wyss, Thelma Hatch.
Here at the Scenic-Vu Motel.

Summary: In his senior year at Idaho's Pineville High School, Jake finds himself in charge of six other teenagers who must board at the tacky Scenic-Vu Motel, since they live too far from town to commute from their homes to school every day.
[1. Hotels, motels, etc.—Fiction. 2. High schools—Fiction. 3. Schools—Fiction. 4. Idaho—Fiction]
I. Title.
PZ7.W998He 1988   [Fic]   87-45308
ISBN 0-06-022250-6
ISBN 0-06-022251-4 (lib. bdg.)
ISBN 0-06-447001-6 (pbk.)

First Harper Keypoint edition, 1989.
Harper Keypoint is an imprint of HarperTrophy

For my son
David

I

Tuesday, September 4

Here we are at the Scenic-Vu Motel in downtown Pineville, Idaho, where every teenage boy has a Ford pickup truck—except me and the other three Dudes from Bear Flats who are sitting here in Room 9 trying to locate the advertised view.

My name is Jacob R. Callahan—Jake for short—and the other three Dudes you will get to know soon enough.

To begin with, I should clarify that we are not here for the view, *irregardless*, as my dad would say, of the brightest neon sign in town flashing SCENIC-VU, SCENIC-VU, temporarily blinding motorists on Highway 30, and lighting up a good portion of Pineville's Main Street—one and the same.

In addition the red glow illuminates a yard of farm

1

implements to the east, and an empty lot of tumble-weeds and sunflowers to the west.

That red glow, no doubt, also flashes into the bedroom windows of a good number of teenagers in Pineville, as it flashes through the flowered draperies into Room 9. I can't say for certain though, since I have never been in one teenager's bedroom in this town or, for that matter, in their living rooms or kitchens.

Directly in front of the neon sign a scrubby cedar tree stands alone in a patch of gravel. It tilts west, stunted no doubt by the neon rays. That lone tree could be the intended view, but then this place would have been named Cedar-Vu rather than Scenic-Vu.

But it does make a person curious.

"There she is," my brother Jordy exclaimed, nodding toward the office at the east end of the motel. "Mrs. Scenic-Vu herself, standing on her doorstep, flagging down motorists!"

The four of us watched through the window.

"The Big Vu," I said sarcastically. "You know she collects grasshoppers in that net on her head?"

The others burst out laughing and fell back on the two queen-size beds, whose geometric bedspreads clashed with the flowered draperies.

"Let's tell the girls," Drift yelled. "Let's go tell them the Big Vu collects grasshoppers."

Next door in Room 8 the three Dudettes from Bear Flats were no doubt doing the same thing we were—zooming in on the view.

Drift rushed to the door, then back again to the bed. "I can't go out there," he said. "The Big Vu intimidates me!" He ducked his head in a pillow and howled. Drift is fourteen. And loud.

This morning at sunrise Mrs. Scenic-Vu had waved our school bus into her parking lot. When I first saw her signaling in her long multicolored bathrobe and lavender net warbonnet, I thought perhaps she was a nightmare.

The seven of us from Bear Flats tumbled out of the bus with our bags, weary from the one-and-a-half-hour ride to town. As we stepped down on her parking lot, Mrs. Scenic-Vu emitted a sharp scream like a mechanical mouse.

"Male *and* female!" she screeched. "I do not approve." She clutched the collar of her bathrobe as if choking herself.

We returned her look of horror.

"This will never work," she moaned, "even if the board of education says it will. The board of education doesn't know everything. The board of education doesn't know anything. Oh why, oh why, did they pick on me? Why not the Uptown? Why, oh why?" She gasped for air and released her collar.

Because I am the oldest, seventeen, and in charge of this crazy group, I spoke up. "We have rules to follow, Mrs. —"

"Rules, rules. Nobody follows rules anymore," she snapped. "Not even the board of education." She waved for us to follow.

"And I'm warning you right now," she continued. "If I catch one male in the females' room or one female

in the males' room, you'll be out in this parking lot—
on your heads!"

"Oh, shucks!" Drift rubbed his head and rolled his
eyes upward.

I frowned at him. This was no way to get along with
our new landlady.

We followed her across the parking lot to a covered
sidewalk stretching the length of the faded green motel.

"Males wait here," she ordered. She ushered the
three girls into Room 8 and closed the door.

She reappeared after a few minutes, smiling a pinched
little smile. "Males follow me," she hissed.

We followed her into the end room.

"The room is large," she said gesturing grandly.
"And comfortable. The bath"—she waved vaguely—
"and the kitchenette.

"Not the Plaza," she quipped, opening the draperies
so we could see what she was talking and waving about,
"but a close second. The Plaza of Pineville, let's say."

"If you say so," Martin said wearily. He took off his
cowboy hat, scratched his head, and put his hat back
on.

Mrs. Scenic-Vu bristled. "This is not going to work,
just like I said it wouldn't. Tell me why the board of
education picked on me. Why not the Uptown? Why,
why, why?"

She was looking directly at my brother Jordy, so he
gave the first answer that popped into his fourteen-
year-old mind.

"Because you have hot plates," he said. "Kitchen-
ettes, you call them."

4

Mrs. Scenic-Vu gasped.

"And it will help pay for your big neon sign," I added, a remark that was uncalled for, but under the circumstances very gratifying.

We seven Males and Females from Bear Flats are here at the Scenic-Vu Motel compliments of the Board of Education of Pine Valley School District. The only reason I am writing any of this down is because my senior English teacher assigned it.

Hello, Mrs. Christensen!

I might as well tell you in the beginning, I don't believe in keeping journals unless a person is famous or something, which I am not. Let famous people record their daily thoughts and actions for self-discovery or posterity.

But not me. I have enough problems just being Jacob R. Callahan from Bear Flats without writing any of it down. But of course, Mrs. Christensen, I do believe in graduating next spring from Pine Valley High School.

So here goes! I guess you want what my dad calls "the straight poop." That's one of his grosser phrases. Another is "crap," as in crap motel. He used both of them in the school board meeting last week, as anyone who reads the *Pineville Weekly News* knows.

The headlines the next day read: BEAR FLATTERS WANT "STRAIGHT POOP," BOARD OF EDUCATION TOLD.

That's my dad, all right—the one and only George F. Callahan. He attends a simple school board meeting, and he makes the headlines.

Ten families live up on the mountain at Bear Flats,

5

but this year only Dad attended the board meeting. The perpetual discussion with the board over high school education is not a trivial concern for the parents of Bear Flats. It is, in fact, a major problem. They just get tired year after year of worrying about it and making the trip down to attend the board of education meetings.

When my dad came down last week, he was just as weary of the problem as everyone else, and he did not plan to sit around arguing all night. He was tired of discussing a permanent problem that year after year receives a temporary solution.

"Just give us the straight poop," he said to the board.

After a strained silence, the board president, Horace Leander, read this year's decree:

There will be no daily school bus to Bear Flats as in the distant past. There will be no private boardinghouses as in the recent past. There *will* be a school bus to and from Bear Flats two days a week: Monday A.M. and Friday P.M., weather and roads permitting.

"And between Monday A.M. and Friday P.M.?" my dad roared.

"There is a motel—"

"A crap motel?"

"A motel for which the board of education has arranged to pay one hundred dollars per student per month, because no one wants to drive a bus up Big Bear Canyon and no one wants to board teenagers.

"And this is the final decision of the board of education until the citizens of Bear Flats are willing to move down to civilization."

So here we are, staying four nights a week at the Scenic-Vu Motel, or as my dad would say, the crap motel.

The Females in Room 8 are:

Mona Robbins, 16
Netty Robbins, 14
Helen Burgoyne, 14

The Males in Room 9 are:

Martin Rawley, 16
Drift Davis, 14
Jordon Callahan, 14
and yours truly, the journalist, Jake Callahan, 17

Well, Mrs. Christensen, how is this for the first day of school?

II

Wednesday, September 5

Pineville girls are cuter than Bear Flatters! I think
it's their hair.

Thursday, September 6

Describe myself, Mrs. Christensen? The real me? Only
because you say our journals will be locked in a file,
not to be read even by yourself until next spring. After
that we can go away to college or fly off into space,
never to return to Pineville, Idaho. Is that the idea,
Mrs. C.?

Well, here goes. My name is Jake Callahan, as
everyone knows by now, and I am a senior at Pine

Valley High School. I have been going to this high school for four years now, from a different address each year. Maybe that's the reason everyone knows my name—and just my name.

"Hi, Jake." "Hi, Callahan," they say.

After four years wouldn't you think someone would expand? "Hi, Jake. Want to come over tonight and study math?" Or English. Or history or biology.

What I think about most is cruising Main Street in a Ford pickup truck, an F-250 four-wheel drive with a stick shift. With big mud tires, a roll bar, and four KC Daylighters on top. All decked out. Maybe even a gun rack inside the cab, and a stereo playing country music.

Also I think about girls—town girls to take home after school, town girls to ride next to me in the cab of my pickup, or in the back, or leaning on the roll bar. Or for that matter, all over the darn thing.

Beautiful town girls with blond hair bouncing on their shoulders, with names like Jinny, Amber, and Blythe. Names that whisper of love.

I was hoping to have a chance with one of them this year, but so far I have been followed around by three scared and skinny Dudettes with names only a Bear Flats mother would name a daughter: Mona, Netty, and Helen.

In other words, Mona the Short, Netty the Tall, and Helen of Troy. Even without names you can tell they are from Bear Flats, a trio walking arm in arm, giggling. And the scareder they get, the more they giggle.

On the outside I'm just regular—tall and thin and good at sports, especially running. But as you know,

Mrs. C., at Pine Valley High School it's football and basketball. The coach said I wouldn't be at all bad on the football team if I could get down for summer practice. As it is, he feels obligated to put the town dudes on the team because he is training them, and they can get to summer practice. It's the same with basketball.

I practice a lot on my own though. During the summer I ran five miles every morning before working on our place. And last year while I was boarding with Mrs. Whitely, I ran two miles to and from school each day. Besides all the errands she ran me on.

The day school closed last May, she moved out of town and took along all that board of education money she had earned on me.

Anyway, I get in a lot of running, just living.

Meanwhile, back at the motel—
This is not a motel, a home on the highway. This is a madhouse! The TV is on high volume to drown out the TV on high volume in Room 8. Steam is pouring out of the bathroom where Martin has been showering for twenty minutes already.

Drift and Jordy are passing a football from bed to bed because the potato chips on the carpet hurt their feet. We are all waiting for Martin to get out of the shower because it is his turn to cook supper.

Martin is staying in the shower because he doesn't know how to cook any better than the rest of us. He thinks if he stays in there long enough, someone will do it for him.

Martin also thinks he is a psychologist. Up in Bear Flats he hypnotizes chickens. He grabs a hen, draws an arrow on the ground, and tells the hen to look at it. It gets them every time. Whenever Martin comes over to our place, my mother says, "Keep him away from the chickens."

I seem to remember that I am the oldest and in charge of this mess. If this is the responsibility that comes with age, I'll be senile before I am eighteen.

I made only two rules, but these Dudes cannot even follow two rules. I guess I will have to call a meeting. And we just had one on Tuesday.

Last week after the school board meeting, Dad reported to the Bear Flatters assembled on our front lawn. He waved his arms and shouted, *"Irregardless* of their college diplomas, they have made one more stupid decision."

All the parents said aye to that.

Then Dad turned to me. "You're the oldest, Jake. You will have to be responsible. You will have to enforce the rules. So take my advice and make a short list."

When the school bus pulled up Tuesday morning, he patted me on the back and said the same thing he says every year: "Now Jake, my boy, study hard and have fun."

So I made those the rules: 1. Study Hard. 2. Have Fun.

Now I am wondering if his advice is so great, considering that he ended up on a run-down farm on the

11

side of a mountain called Bear Flats. Shouting *irre-gardless* at everyone.

Maybe that's my main problem—trying to follow those two stupid rules of his for the past three years.

He should move down here to Pineville with his shaggy beard and ponytail down his back and try to live his own rules in civilization.

He and gray-haired Angel with him. (Angel is my mom, and short for Angel of Doom.) The two of them are free as the birds. Dropouts from the mainstream of life, some people say. More accurately, relics of the sixties.

Don't get me wrong, Mrs. Christensen. They are not anti-American. They vote. They work hard on their forty acres and mind their own business and expect everyone else to do the same.

They don't ask for help. They do not write their congressman, and they do not write the president. However, if the president of the United States wrote them a letter, they would gladly reply. They could tell him a thing or two, just as they tell the board of education.

Dad would wave the president's letter around and shout incoherent patriotic eulogies through his beard. Then Angel would answer it without pomp or circumstance, without notifying her next-door neighbor or the *Pineville Weekly News*.

Sitting in her hammock, she would write the president a chatty letter on the back of his and tell him a military secret or two; namely, about the Russians coming across the Bering Strait down into Idaho. She would warn him of assassins and ask if he has a year's supply of food in his basement. At the end she would add a P.S.: Zola sends her love.

Zola, Mrs. Christensen, is the wife of a college history professor for whom Angel worked as a secretary one summer. He dictated letters all summer long, always concluding with the postscript: Zola sends her love.

Angel uses it exclusively now.

Last Tuesday I presented the two rules to the Dudes and Dudettes at a meeting in the Scenic-Vu office. With Mrs. Scenic-Vu eavesdropping at her desk, we did not have to worry about ending up in the parking lot on our heads. Also there was an upright Naugahyde sofa.

"There are only two rules," I told them. "Study Hard and Have Fun."

"Just two?" Mona the Short asked skeptically. She sat curled up on the sofa with Netty the Tall and Helen of Troy and a large bag of potato chips.

"Just two," I repeated. "Think about them for a minute and then we will vote."

"What's there to think about?" Drift said. "I'm brainwashed already."

"Those are two awesome rules," Martin drawled.

"All right," I said. "All in favor say aye."

They all said aye.

"Opposed?" There was silence.

"The ayes have it," I said. "Meeting adjourned."

"Three cheers for the chairman," Mona the Short yelled. She leaped from the sofa right into a cheer—down on the floor, up in the air. "Rah, rah, rah!"

"Pass the potato chips," Jordy shouted.

Helen of Troy tossed the potato chips to Jordy, and missed. Everyone rushed out the door.

"Thanks for the use of the office, Mrs. —" I mumbled, picking up the potato chip bag.

I should have known it all went too easy.

Just now I received a wet stocking in my face. Time for another meeting!

III

Friday, September 7

As I have said before, Mrs. Christensen, I have enough problems of my own just being Jacob R. Callahan. Yet here I am Chairman of the Social Misfits.

These kids all wear faded Levi's, sweatshirts, and cowboy boots. They all have equal shares of freckles, braces, glasses, and zits. At times they can be smart and real cool. And sometimes funny as a rubber crutch. (A George F. Callahan simile.) Other times they act like—sentence fragments. (A Jacob R. Callahan original.)

They would be perfectly normal teenagers *if* they lived in Pineville.

* * *

"All right, you Bear Flatters," I told them at the meeting. "Only two rules and you can't keep them. What are you, slobs?"

Mona, Netty, and Helen looked up sleepily from the sofa where they had dumped themselves. Maybe it was their hair hanging down in their eyes that made them look sleepy.

Mona and Netty are sisters who look like twins except Mona is sixteen and short, and Netty is fourteen and tall. You would think it would be just the other way around. Together they have yards of black hair.

Helen has blond hair that hangs down over her glasses like roller blinds. She definitely needs a haircut. She also needs to throw away an ambiguous stuffed animal named Ralphy that she drags around.

The boys sat on the floor, leaning against the sofa with their cowboy hats propped on their knees—except for Martin, who always wears his, showering excluded. He says it keeps his brain cells from wandering.

"I've been keeping Rule Two," Drift announced. "I've been having lots of fun!"

Drift is the one with the braces and most of the freckles. The smart aleck with the big mouth.

(Remember, I said you would meet them soon enough.)

Drift has always been treated a little special in Bear Flats because he was born in a car stuck in a snowdrift halfway between Bear Flats and Pineville. It was a smart-aleck thing for a baby to do and he deserved his name. Whenever he passes that spot in the road, he puts his right hand over his heart and observes a moment of silence. He is going to build a shrine there as soon as he gets enough money.

"Playing the TV while I was trying to study was fun for you, Drift, but not for me," I said. "Squirting water from a plastic bag was fun for you, but it ruined Martin's history map. Potato chips in Jordy's bed—"

"Hey, no fair, Dude."

"We are all in this motel together. Remember?"

The girls snickered and fiddled with their yards of hair.

"And the girls are worse!" I said. "They watch the late movie every night and fall asleep before it's over. We hear it all night long in our room."

"There's no rule against TV!" Mona the Short said, waking up.

"Study Hard," I quoted. "Rule One. How do you Bear Flatters think you are going to make the honor roll?"

"Nobody said anything about the honor roll," Drift said, grimacing.

"What do you think 'Study Hard' means? Do you freshmen need everything spelled out in detail?"

They were all wide-awake now.

"Whose side are you on, anyway?" Jordy asked, squirming uncomfortably. This was hard on a little brother.

"Our side," I said. "Why do you think I kept the rules down to two? We must have rules. Everyone says so—the board of education, our parents, Mrs. Scenic-Vu."

"Let's turn those two in for two others," Netty suggested. She is tall even when she is sitting down.

"Name two," I said, "that everyone will agree on."

"What about 'Have Fun' and 'Have More Fun'?" Martin suggested. (Everybody's a smart aleck.)

"Redundant," I said.

There were no other suggestions.

"All right, Bear Flatters," I continued, "do you want to hear, as my dad would say—"

"Sure, give us the straight poop," Drift said. (Everybody reads the *Pineville Weekly News*.)

"All right," I said. "Shape up or ship out of this motel."

"Where to?" Helen piped up.

"That's the point," I said. "This motel is the last place, the very last place the board of education could come up with. Don't expect anything better than this."

"What about the Uptown?" Jordy asked.

"We will ignore that remark, Jordy, because you are a freshman."

"I just remembered," Jordy said. "The Uptown doesn't have hot plates."

"We must accept the fact," I said, "that the board of education has used all of its alternatives. Last year it was boardinghouses for three of us.

"I boarded with Mrs. Whitely two miles north of town. As soon as I ran there after school, she would send me on an errand back to town—to pay her phone bill, to pick up a prescription at the drugstore—all by foot, you understand. Rain or snow.

"Martin boarded with some alcoholics who lived over the pool hall, and he was late for school every day of the year. He was lucky to receive credit for his sophomore year."

Martin concurred by holding his nose.

"Why were you always late, Martin?"

"Cooking breakfast for them."

"Cooking breakfast for alcoholics!"

I looked over at Mona on the sofa. "What did you do last year?"

"Mrs. MacCallister had seven children. I had to tend them all the time." She pulled a face.

"The other alternative," I said, "is busing. One and a half hours before school each morning and the same after school each night. Three hours a day cooped up in a school bus—besides school all day."

There was silence in the office.

Martin adjusted his hat. "I vote for the two rules. What about the rest of you?"

They all nodded and said, "Aye."

Helen asked, "If we can't do our homework can we watch TV?"

"No TV until after homework. Why can't you do your homework?"

"I don't understand math. My dad always helped me at home."

"I will help you every night."

Helen's face lit up like a Christmas tree. (How is that for a simile, Mrs. Christensen?) "Where? I can't go in your room and you can't come in mine. I'm a Female and you're—"

We all glanced over at Mrs. Scenic-Vu sitting at her desk, nodding and shaking her warbonnet as she agreed or disagreed.

She bubbled forth like a fountain. (Another simile here.) "You can have your tutoring sessions here in

19

the office. And I won't turn on the TV while you are studying. I just turn it on out of habit anyway. I had teenagers once. Almost forgot they couldn't all do math. One could do it like a whiz, but couldn't diagram a sentence. That was Homer. Now my Polly couldn't understand math and couldn't sew a straight seam in home ec class, either. Almost worried me and her dad to death. But she got married just fine—"

"Thanks, Mrs. —"

"Mrs. Matz. M-a-t-z. Say it two or three times."

"Mrs. Matz—"

Drift repeated, "Mrs. Matz, Mrs. Matz, Mrs. Matz. Got it!"

"Anyone who needs help with homework come to the office," I said. "Everyone else study hard in your own room. We are all in this motel together. Any comments?"

"Is the meeting over?" Jordy asked.

"Everyone in favor say aye."

"Aye."

"Meeting adjourned."

If I can get Motel Management taken care of, maybe I can start working on Popularity at School: go to a football game and a stomp, cruise Main with the guys, and maybe help Jinny Thornwall with her math at her house.

IV

Monday, September 10

This morning Mrs. Matz was waiting on her doorstep in her bathrobe, smiling. Good grief, did she miss us over the weekend?

I missed Jinny Thornwall. I have been dreaming of Jinny Thornwall for three years, ever since I sat behind her in freshman math. All year long her beautiful hair bounced on her shoulders like golden Ping-Pong balls.

This year she sits across the aisle from me in English. Her profile— But of course, Mrs. C., you know Jinny Thornwall.

Angel sent cold roast beef left over from Sunday.

Angel says motels burn down in the night.

After school we all walked up to Food King for groceries. We Dudes each bought for one night. The Dudettes shop and cook in trio, naturally. Looks like hot dogs and potato chips in both rooms this week.

Tuesday, September 11

Jordy walked in his sleep last night. I found him out on Highway 30 in his shorts. Angel has been worrying about this, afraid some weirdo will pick him up. Now I'm worried.

The problem is that Jordy tries to act like Drift, the smart aleck. But he can't pull it off because he was born a poet. And I am sorry to say this, Mrs. C., but in this world, no one needs a poet.

Would you believe I can read Jordy's face before he says a word? Now that's what I call a handicap. He is like Dad. You wouldn't guess that about my dad with all his waving and shouting at the board of education, but that's because you don't really know him. The reason he moved up to Bear Flats is because he was born a poet, too.

Jordy is smart, though. Smart enough not to ask about all my girlfriends I told him about last year. And cruising Main with the guys.

He said to me the other night when Martin and Drift were asleep, "If sometimes this year I act like a regular person, rather than your little brother, do you understand?"

I said I understood. See what I mean?

Wednesday, September 12

Just before dark Jordy walked over to the window to pull the draperies. "What is Mona doing on the driveway?" he exclaimed. "Directing traffic?"

We all rushed over to look.

"She has gone mad," Martin said. "Completely mad."

"Mad Mona," Drift said gleefully. He rubbed his hands together.

"She is practicing for Pep Club tryouts," I said. "All junior girls do. Now pull the draperies."

Thursday, September 13

I would like to stay over for the football game and the stomp Friday night, but I don't want to go alone.

The Dudes want to go home for a good meal and clean clothes. They need to go home; they are regular pigs.

I asked Martin tonight, as we wiped down the kitchenette, where he learned to cook spaghetti. He said he had just learned tonight!

Monday, September 17

Mona the Short is trying out for Pep Club. All the junior girls are trying out—cheering and jumping and strutting around the halls of good old Pine Valley High School. Only twenty-five are accepted, so it's a real big deal.

Today at noon they all marched around the football field for the first round of judging. All the boys skipped lunch and sat in the bleachers and whistled.

This kid I know from auto mechanics, Joe Grant, came over and sat down by me. "Lots of cute legs, huh?" he said.

"You can say that again," I said.

Tuesday, September 18

Today the girls brought scrapbooks, of what content I do not know. They were piled up on the front of the stage in the auditorium. The boys couldn't go in and look because Miss Owens stationed herself at the double doors in the back.

All I know is that Mona's scrapbook was so heavy she couldn't carry it herself. So guess who carried it? And when I asked what was inside, she said it was none of my business.

Wednesday, September 19

Pep Club tryouts continue.

Mona continues jumping on Mrs. Matz's driveway, behind her compact car. Netty the Tall and Helen of Troy sit on the back bumper of the compact car.

"She'll wear out her boots," Jordy remarks from the window.

"Her lungs," Martin says.

Thursday, September 20

Today must be Pompon Day. Purple-and-White Crepe Paper Pompon Day.

Junior girls are cute!

Friday, September 21

We all went to the Pep Club assembly today. We all sat together—all the Bear Flatters, I mean—except Mona, who was up on the stage standing in a line of scared girls that doubled back across the stage two or three times.

One at a time each girl stepped forward and led the students in a cheer:

> *"We're from Pine Valley,*
> *Couldn't be prouder;*
> *If you can't hear us now,*
> *We'll yell a little louder!*
> *Rah, rah, rah!"*

"All those smiles look the same to me," Jordy whispered in my ear.

"Look at the legs," I whispered back.

After school I hurried down to the office to read the bulletin board, but I could not get near it. Girls were all over the place, hugging each other, laughing and crying.

But not Mona.

I waited impatiently at the front door with the other

25

Bear Flatters. "Where is she?" I kept asking Netty and Helen.

"She didn't make it," Netty said, her voice faltering. "She didn't make it."

"Go on to the motel," I told them. "But don't get on the bus, *irregardless* of what Mr. Bernelli says. I'll wait for Mona."

When the office cleared out, I went in and checked the bulletin board. I read the list over and over—half a dozen times—but Mona's name was not there.

I ran upstairs, past the girls' lockers and down to the girls' room at the end of the hall. I leaned against the radiator in front of the window and waited.

Some girls went by. A couple of them waved and said, "See ya, Jake."

I said, "Sure."

Gradually the hall cleared out, and I was about the only one left.

Then here came big Budd Swaney down the hall. Big man on the Pine Valley High School football team. He was headed for the radiator, but when he saw I was there, he changed his mind and leaned against the lockers instead.

We looked at each other, but didn't say anything. He seemed to be talking to himself, though, telling himself how fine he looked in his white pants and pink shirt.

Two junior girls came out of the girls' room, trailing purple and white pompons. They sashayed over to big Budd Swaney, who swooped them up, one in each arm, and walked off down the hall and down the stairs.

The girls laughed and squealed, shaking their pompons over his head.

I don't think I like Budd Swaney—or his white pants.

Finally Mona came out of the girls' room, clutching her backpack to her chest. She had pulled her long hair over her red eyes, so she could hardly see where she was going. She jumped when she saw me at the radiator.

"What are you doing here?" she asked.

"Waiting for you."

"I don't need a chaperon," she snapped.

"I know that," I said, taking her arm. "Let's get out of here."

Crossing the lawn she said, "I didn't make Pep Club."

"I read the bulletin board," I said. "You can't out-guess judges."

"They weren't judges, really," Mona said, quavering. "Just the officers and Miss Owens. But just the officers, really. They mostly choose their friends, even though Miss Owens makes them go through the formalities."

I nodded and took her backpack.

To make her feel better I said, "You did look good in the assembly, Mona. Your legs and all looked good."

"Thanks," she whispered. "But I still didn't make it."

"I know. But your legs and all looked real good."

She looked up and smiled quickly. And we both took off running down the sidewalk.

V

Monday, September 24

Angel sent roast beef for supper.

Angel says motels always get robbed.

Tuesday, September 25

Hot dogs. Drift's turn to cook.

Yes, Mrs. Christensen, it probably is a good idea that you call for our journals monthly, because where would I keep a thing like this? As it is, I carry it with me almost all the time, to protect myself.

Yes, Mrs. Christensen, it probably is another good idea for you to scan them each month for pornography before locking them in the file. I can understand you might not want to graduate someone who has spent an entire year writing pornography for your English class. The last laugh, and all that.

And yes, Mrs. Christensen, I am trying my best to glorify the beloved language by using an occasional metaphor.

Wednesday, September 26

I cook a great hamburger.

By the way, Mrs. Christensen, are you related to anyone on the board of education?

Thursday, September 27

Well, Mrs. C., we have another big problem in this motel: junk food. Junk food on the table, under the table, on the bed, under the bed, etc.

I may have to call another meeting.

Every night I help the Dudettes with their math and the Dudes with science—except Martin. But then, he keeps his hat on. I wish someone would help me with this journal. Someone named Jinny Thornwall.

I told the girls tonight that the reason they have trouble with math is because of all the potato chips they consume. Bag after bag.

If you want to know the truth, Mrs. C., *irregardless* of what you say, I cannot see what good this journal is going to do me. I think it is a waste of time and paper. I want to get rid of my problems, not write them down for posterity. And this journal is one of my problems.

Monday, October 1

Tall girls are really noticeable. Especially tall girls with black hair flying all over the place who wave at me at school. Like Netty the Tall.

Today, for example, when we passed in the hall she did it again.

She screeched. "Hi, Jake. You'll be glad to hear what I got in math today!"

Everyone hears. Everyone looks.

"She your sister?" this kid named Mike Harvey asked one day after chemistry.

"No," I said. "Not my sister."

"Tall drink of water, isn't she?" He guffawed so everyone, including Netty, could hear.

"Tall and beautiful," I said, waving back at Netty. "Her mother is a fashion model; her dad is an Olympic triathlon coach. And she is only a freshman."

"Oh, yeah?" Mike turned around for another look, but Netty the Tall had turned the corner.

Tuesday, October 2

If no one in this motel eats Twinkies, how do all these sticky wrappers get in?

Tonight Jordy said, "I'm worried about Angel."

"Why?"

"Because I think she is worried about us. Last year she worried about you out at Mrs. Whitely's—getting poisoned from her food, reading her dirty literature. Once she sat in the car for three hours in a snowstorm determined to drive down here to Pineville. I just wonder what she does with both of us away."

"She worries about the motel burning down."

"And robbers."

"And Peeping Toms."

"Perverts."

"Do you think we're safe here, Jake? Right on Highway 30?"

"With Mrs. Matz standing on her front steps? I think she stands there all night."

"I hope so," Jordy said. He rolled over and went to sleep.

Good old Angel, who used to be just the typical Angel Mom—playing her guitar, singing ballads, and swinging with us in a hammock on the porch.

I wonder when she realized that Dad was never going to provide for ordinary mainstream Pineville America, with the winter town house, the Ford pickup truck. I wonder when she realized she was trapped up a canyon at a place called Bear Flats with a poet and two children.

I don't remember when it was, but I remember she changed. She started to worry and warn and cry in the hammock. And now I can hardly remember her any other way.

Wednesday, October 3

If no one in this motel drinks pop, how does the bathtub fill up with pop cans?

Thursday, October 4

I walk on potato chips. I sit on potato chips. And I sleep on potato chips!

Some kids won't learn any other way. I called another meeting.

At supper I told the Dudes to meet in the office at seven o'clock sharp or they knew where they would end up—on their heads—and then I pounded on the door to Room 8.

"Ramona Lisa! Marie Antoinetty! Helen of Troy! The motel's on fire. Meet in the office immediately. Unclothed, if possible!"

The door opened and a soggy towel hit me in the face.

In the office I roared at them. "All right, you Bear Flatters. Do you like meetings? Do you want more rules? Are you still slobs?"

"What is this meeting about?" Martin demanded. "I have never studied so hard in my whole life."

"Junk food."

"There's no rule against junk food," Drift shouted. "I have them memorized: Study Hard and Have Fun." He grinned at everyone.

Mrs. Matz scurried in breathlessly and sat down at her desk as if she were late for school. She began nodding and shaking her warbonnet. (The grasshoppers inside are hair curlers.)

"Here I go explaining the obvious again for the freshmen. Rule One: Study Hard. There is no way you can study hard with salt on your brains."

"Salt on my brain?" Helen clutched her head.

"Didn't your mother tell you about salt and cholesterol and preservatives and poisons before you left home?"

"My mother just gave me a big kiss," Mona said, sighing dramatically, "and said it was a cold, cruel world."

"I don't suppose you Dudettes will be able to finish school this year," I said.

"And why not?" Netty asked. She was unwrapping a Twinkie.

"If you keep eating Twinkies at the rate you are going, you won't be able to get through the school door."

The boys roared.

"Besides rotten teeth and bad breath."

"Give us a break, please," Mona pleaded.

"No breaks. Not with extreme cases. On Monday I will check your shopping carts. Be prepared."

"Give me Monday night and I'll heat up my mom's Sunday roast like Jordy," Drift scoffed.

"You'd burn it, Drift," Jordy retorted.

"We drew days out of Martin's hat. Remember? You drew first, Drift. Remember? You are Tuesday. We will draw again in January."

"Shucks," Drift said. "In this meeting could we decide on a set menu? Say, roast beef on Monday, hot dogs on Tuesday, steak on Wednesday, steak on Thursday—"

(I wonder if all smart alecks have freckles and braces, or if you just notice them on smart alecks when you want to bash in their noses?)

"This meeting is too long," Helen complained. "I need to wash my hair."

"Why don't you wash that animal while you are at it?" Mona said.

"And so," I yelled, and waved my arms, "if Mrs. Matz goes into our rooms this weekend to change the beds and finds potato chips smashed in the carpets, and Twinkies in the closets, and cinnamon bears under the beds—not to mention pop cans in the bathtubs— you know where we will be next Monday."

"The Uptown."

"No, Drift," Jordy corrected. "Not the Uptown. No hot plates."

"Oh, yes. I remember. Shucks!"

"In the parking lot on our heads," Martin said.

"That's right. Meeting adjourned."

I don't have time to do everything twice, Mrs. C.— live it *and* write it down, too. I just have time to live it.

Look at this list, will you:

> Study for chemistry test tomorrow.
> Rewrite history paper for tomorrow.
> Help girls with math.

Help Drift with biology.
Wash out socks and shorts.
Tell Martin to wash his smelly socks.
Remember Parent-Teacher Conference for
   Jordy on Monday.
Remember Jordy has to get more sleep.

VI

Monday, October 8

When Angel gave me a kiss and half a roast this morning, I never thought a day could hold so many problems.

First of all, in the Ford Pickup Capital of the World, it is humiliating to pull up in front of the local high school in a little yellow school bus.

Mr. Bernelli charged the bus up the driveway to the front door, brakes screeching and horn honking, just as the first bell rang. He grinned at us through the rearview mirror, thinking he had done us Bear Flatters one big favor.

For some unexplained reason late this morning, he had rolled down Big Bear Canyon at a speed that would have put Angel right to bed had she known.

"Slow down, bus driver," the girls called. "Slow down. We are getting dusty."

Mr. Bernelli has not swept his bus since the board of education purchased it four years ago. I recognized school bulletins from my sophomore year.

"Here's that release form my mom was supposed to sign two years ago," Martin said, holding up a pink sheet of paper.

"Have her sign it this year," Mona suggested. "I just found a poem I am going to turn in again."

"You know, Mr. Bernelli," I called out, "with all this information, we could go to school in this bus. We could almost graduate in this bus!"

He glanced back through his rearview mirror. Expressionless.

Anyway, one and a half hours later he sped right past the Scenic-Vu, right past Mrs. Matz standing on her doorstep waving her multicolored arms.

"You passed the motel," we all shouted. "Back up. Reverse!"

"You'll be late for school."

"We don't care," I spoke for all. "We've been late before. Turn back."

"And get in trouble with the board of education? No, thanks. I'm getting you kids there before the first bell, and I think I hear it ringing now."

"But our clothes—" Mona called.

"I'll go right back to the motel and unload them in the office," Mr. Bernelli replied.

"Nobody carries my Ralphy," Helen whined, clutching her ugly beast.

"Put him in the bag with your curling iron," Mona said. "You can't take him to school."

"But my mom's roast—" Jordy shouted.

"I'll tell Mrs. Matz to put it in the fridge," Mr. Bernelli said.

By that time we had gone almost two blocks past the motel, and the school was just ahead. We were all grumpy with Mr. Bernelli as we stepped off the bus one by one, like biology specimens delivered in the nick of time.

"Make sure that roast gets in the refrigerator," I snapped.

And there we were on the front steps with half the football team and the cheerleaders—the elite of Pine Valley High School, you could say.

"What's this?" big Budd Swaney said, not looking at us, but smiling real cool at the other kids.

They all smiled real cool smiles at each other, then turned in front of us at the door.

"They ride a little yellow bus," Mike Harvey said, choking a laugh.

They were all muffling laughs as the door swung shut behind them.

After school we Bear Flatters met at the front door as we always do. We walked home to the motel together, not talking, just listening to the fallen leaves wrinkling under our cowboy boots.

Since it was Monday, we deposited our books at the motel, waved to Mrs. Matz, then headed up Main to Food King.

"If you don't want a meeting in Food King," I cautioned as we walked along, "remember our meeting last Thursday. No junk food. Meet at the south checkout."

Every mother in Pineville must have been in that Food King store, pushing carts up and down the aisles like race car drivers.

"Follow a lady who looks like your mom and buy the same things," Martin said. He tugged at a grocery cart wedged in the rack.

"There's nobody in here like my mother," Jordy whispered hoarsely. "Tight pants and streaked hair and fingernail polish . . ."

A lady in tight designer jeans gave him a dirty look as she whizzed by.

I pushed my cart like a race car driver also. To the meat, to the milk, to the lettuce, back to the cottage cheese, to the bread, back to the eggs, back to the tomatoes. I then stationed myself near the south checkout and flipped through a copy of *Woman's Day* while I waited.

I actually had trouble breathing, Mrs. C., when I saw their loaded carts approaching.

"Take out that junk," I ordered.

"Like what?" Drift demanded. He leaned over his cart protectively. "I just followed a happy fat lady."

"To enumerate—" I said, pointing.

"Potato chips—out!

"Sugar-coated cereal—out!

"Refried beans—out!

"Chocolate milk—out!

"Caramel corn—out!

"Six-pack of pop—out!

"Salted peanuts—out!"

"Yes, master," they all chorused. "Yes, master."

They backed their carts around a mammoth paper-towel display, and returned shortly with more nutritious selections. They looked very pleased with themselves.

One thing I will say for Bear Flatters: They can switch from Dumb to Smart real fast.

Now the next part I want to forget.

As we were filing out of the automatic door with our grocery sacks, a Ford pickup pulled up just in front of us. And guess who was at the wheel? Jinny Thornwall, in living color, with two other gorgeous girls in the cab with her.

How lucky can a guy get?

Was it luck, or had she followed me from school, to the motel, to Food King? While all the time I had been listening to autumn leaves wrinkle?

Jinny and her friends bounced out of the pickup and headed toward us. My heart jumped up and grabbed my throat, and my hands began to sweat. But I managed to sound cool when I said, "Hi, Jinny Thornwall in my English class. Need a ride?"

It only took a minute, but in that same minute she whizzed past me like lightning. She heard her name as the door was closing and she glanced back. "Oh," she said, surprised. "Hi."

She did not fly around the divider and jump on the electric eye. She did not wave through the glass doors. She did not even notice me when I was standing right in front of her.

"Forget her," Martin said as we cruised the sidewalk back to the motel. "She is one stuck-up girl."

"Oh, shut up," I said.

40

* * *

Back at the Scenic-Vu, I rushed through my homework and tutoring so I could get over to school for the Parent-Teacher Conference. I was in no mood for the P.T. Conference; I was going for Jordy because Angel had asked me to.

As I walked the three blocks to school, smashing leaves, I started thinking how great it would be if Jordy and I could both be on the honor roll. All year.

Then I started thinking how great it would be if all the Bear Flatters could be on the honor roll all year.

There are some brilliant chemists and poets up at Bear Flats, planting gardens. On sabbatical, you might say. And some of their kids are temporarily camped at the Scenic-Vu Motel. But those kids are brilliant. Those kids are achievers. Those kids are scholars.

The idea kept racing through my head like a song. The more I thought about it, the happier I felt and the faster I walked. When I reached the school, I charged in with the arrogance of the mayor of Pineville.

The teachers were all dressed up, sitting at tables in the cafeteria, and the parents were standing in lines waiting their turns.

I joined Mr. Hudson's line for freshman English, which would take care of two Dudes and two Dudettes all at the same time.

Mr. Hudson said in all his years at Pine Valley High School this was the first P.T. Conference at which Bear Flats had been represented by anyone.

I said, "That's a start. How are we doing?"

Mr. Hudson put on his horn-rimmed reading glasses

and looked into his roll book. "Poorly," he said distastefully, as if something unpleasant had escaped. "Oh, so poorly."

"Why?" I asked. "They are geniuses."

He peered over his glasses at me. "You don't say?"

He frowned into his roll book again. "Homework never turned in," he said, waving me aside. "Next?"

I stood in the general math line for Netty and Helen until I lost courage. Then I changed over to home ec, which I thought would be a cinch.

Miss Fischer said it was really none of my business, but since it needed to be somebody's business, Netty and Helen were both pulling shaky C's.

"Shaky C's?" I exclaimed. "But they love home ec. They don't love math, but they love home ec. They cook every night. Goulash, macaroni and cheese—"

"These F's"—Miss Fischer pointed to two black smudges in her roll book—"are for the cake unit. The cake unit, just last Friday.

"After I spent one week demonstrating the simple process of making and baking a yellow cake, Netty and Helen brought to class a cake baked in a frying pan, which they had to chisel out of the frying pan, giggling all the while, disrupting the entire class—"

"They did not *bake* it," I interrupted. "They fried it. They don't have an oven."

Miss Fischer picked up a little hourglass that looked like a salt shaker. All the salt had trickled down to the bottom. She turned it over, glared at me, and smiled at the parent behind me.

"But you have to admit," I said in desperation, "it was better than buying a Hostess cake at Food King and taking off the cellophane. I heard two or three of the girls—"

"Next," Miss Fischer announced through pursed lips.

That's when I staggered over to your line, Mrs. Christensen. With the exception of your five-minute vote of confidence, for which I thank you, the P.T. Conference was one big depressant.

During those two hours, I got the picture: No one expects much from Bear Flats, and no one has ever been disappointed.

It rounded out my lousy day.

Back at the Scenic-Vu, I was ready to call another meeting. Instead, I borrowed a pair of scissors from Mrs. Matz to cut my toenails. And I cut the TV cords in both rooms, Male and Female.

Tuesday, October 9

No one is speaking to me.

Friday, October 12

I'm glad it's Friday so I can go home to Angel. No one loves me here.

I wonder if things would go better if I had a Ford pickup.

VII

Monday, October 15

Angel's good old roast.

Angel says people in motels get gassed. She has also been worrying about the Russians crossing the Bering Strait and coming down to Idaho before anyone in Washington, D.C., knows they are here.

I told her to write the president.

Tuesday, October 16

Hot dogs. (Good old Drift.)

Again the Bear Flatters have changed from Dumb to Smart real fast. For two weeks now they have come right home from school and started doing their homework. They even do extra-credit assignments like coloring history maps, reading enrichment novels, and interviewing professionals (Mrs. Matz).

Every few hours I have to call time-out to rest their brain cells. I thump on the Dudettes' wall with my boot and shout, "Time-out, you Three Gorgeous Beauty Queens!"

We meet outside and goof off for a while. We pass a football back and forth over the motel, or run around the block, or watch a TV program in the office with Mrs. Matz.

Then back to the books.

You may think this sounds suspicious, Mrs. Christensen, but you don't really know Bear Flatters. Except me. And that is when I am sitting behind a desk listening to you. You see?

Wednesday, October 17

I found out in psychology today that I am weird. Or adopted. I cannot roll my tongue. Everyone in all Miss Millet's classes can roll tongues, and that means everyone in good old Pine Valley High School rolls tongues. Except me.

Everyone laughed, of course. Miss Millet said it was inherited. She said some people inherit second toes longer than their first, and no lobes on their ears. Not the same people usually.

I hate psychology.

Thursday, October 18

Spaghetti all over. Maybe if Martin took off his cowboy hat, he could see what he was cooking.

Martin is one cool Dude. He has been my friend as long as I can remember, not because we are alike—which we are not—but because we are neighbors up in Bear Flats.

He is built stocky like a tank, and he would be great on the football team if summer practice did not interfere. He has curly blond hair, which not many people see because he always wears his hat. All Bear Flatters wear cowboy hats, although not always indoors. Martin says he likes to keep his brain cells home where they belong.

He also has stinky feet, and he has to get up in the night to move his socks out of the room. He has to because we make him.

(Is this the authenticity you speak of, Mrs. Christensen?)

This afternoon while reading on the bed, he looked up and gazed out the window at the flashing neon sign.

"Ever wonder why this motel was *not* named the Riverside Motel?"

"No river," Drift answered smartly.

"Ever wonder why this motel *was* named the Scenic-Vu?" Martin drawled.

As I said, Martin is one cool Dude.

Friday, October 19

Drift wants to be an astronaut. Would you believe a smart aleck in space?

Monday, October 22

Dad rolls his tongue. Angel rolls hers. I hate psychology.

Tuesday, October 23

Stakeout at Pine Valley girls' room again. This time for Helen of Troy.

Today after school we Bear Flatters met at the front door and waited and waited. No Helen of Troy.

"Where is she?" I complained. "Netty, where is she?"

"Why am I always responsible?" Netty asked. "Okay—there was a note dropped in her locker."

"What did it say?"

"It said, *Meet me at locker 27 after school. You Know Who.*"

"And you let her go alone?"

"She didn't want me to go with her."

"Go on home," I told the others. "I'll find her."

I ran up the stairs, past the girls' lockers, and over to the radiator. Expecting a wait, I pulled out my U.S. history book from my backpack and began reading.

Half a chapter later Helen came out. She did not look good. Skinny and shapeless with braces and glasses.

Big red eyes under the glasses, and bangs hanging over them.

I didn't need to ask the problem. I just took her hand and hurried her down the hall.

Outside I asked, "Who was *You Know Who*?"

"Mike Harvey."

I groaned. "What did he have to say for himself?"

"He just shrieked."

"I guess he dropped the note in the wrong locker," I said.

"I guess so."

"He isn't too smart."

"I guess not."

"So"—I shifted my backpack—"why cry in the girls' room?"

"You wouldn't understand."

"Try me," I said. "I was once a lowly freshman."

"Nobody likes me. Except my Ralphy."

"And *he* is a bore."

Helen stifled a cry, and stomped ahead of me. "I knew you wouldn't understand."

"Oh, I understand, all right," I said. "I understand a lot more than old stuffed Ralphy. I just don't know the answers."

"I don't either."

"What do you say we end this conversation, and run? Until we know the answers?"

Helen nodded. And we took off running down Elm Street. Making a great noise on the pavement.

Thursday, October 25

I have read about people who have dedicated their entire lives to serving others. I am not one of them.

But I did take some time out for Ramona Lisa Robbins this month, because as I have said before, we are all in this motel together. If one goes out on her head, we all go out on our heads.

Dumb Mona. She nearly burned down the motel, just as Angel warned.

Mona told Helen that she had to take her stuffed beast to the cleaners or wash it. Within three days. Or else.

I don't blame Mona. I stay upwind from it when I help Helen with math. It looks contagious.

Helen said she had never slept a night in her entire life without the beast, and that her parents could verify it. She would not send it to the cleaners and she would not wash it.

Last night Mona got up in the middle of the night and kidnaped it out of Helen's arms and went into the bathroom and washed it. Fourteen years of dirt and germs washed out, and it turned out to be a black-and-white dog.

Mona hung it over the tub by its ears.

We all heard Helen scream this morning, including Mrs. Matz and all her unhappy guests in Rooms 4, 5, and 6.

Mrs. Matz charged into Room 8, while we Dudes stood transfixed in the doorway.

Helen was screaming her head off, and Mona was

ironing the dog on her bed with an old iron she had found in the kitchenette.

Mona ironed and chanted mechanically. "I cannot apologize. I did it for Ralphy. Look at him now. He's smiling. He's happy because he is clean. I cannot apologize. I did it for Ralphy."

Mrs. Matz waved her multicolored arms. "Hush up, Helen," she cried. "So that thing was a puppy. Let's put him in my clothes dryer and he'll be dry in no time."

"My hair blower," Mona said suddenly. She ran to the bathroom with the soggy dog and forgot the iron.

"You'll be late for school," Mrs. Matz called. "Go, go, go. Put the little beast on the vanity and he'll be dry when you get home."

We Dudes ducked out fast. I have never seen such waving of arms and screaming over such a minor problem.

Now waving and screaming over a motel burning down is another matter, and that was what Mrs. Matz was doing later.

Helen ran home from school ahead of all of us, and when she threw open the door of Room 8, small flames were darting upward from Mona and Netty's bed. She screamed for Mrs. Matz.

Poor Mrs. Matz. She was just beginning to smile when we pulled up on Monday mornings.

Now she was waving and screaming and throwing buckets of water. "I knew it would never work. I told the board of education it would not work. This is all I need in the *Pineville Weekly News*: TEENAGERS BURN DOWN MOTEL."

She clutched her collar with one hand and covered her eyes with the other. "Oh, my dear Carter, why didn't we buy a Laundromat? Why? Why? Why?"

"I don't know," Mona cried, "but I wish you had. I am so sorry. And I hate that dog. I hate Helen."

I checked the damaged bed. "One blanket, two sheets, one mattress cover, and one mattress. How much, Mrs. Matz?"

"The board of education can figure that out, I am sure," she said. "And I have insurance. My dear Carter saw to that. Oh, how I miss him."

"But if you don't tell the board of education or the insurance or our parents—how much?"

"Not tell the board of education?"

"They would just advertise it," I said. "I don't suppose many travelers would feel like stopping at a motel if they knew the board of education had turned it into a youth hostel. It is not the sort of home on the highway that salesmen or honeymooners—"

"Enough, enough," wailed Mrs. Matz.

"It's too good not to tell," Drift said.

"Not necessarily," Martin the psychologist said. "Mona, will you type this report for me? Mona, will you rub my feet?"

"Got it," Drift said. "I'm not telling a soul."

"I'll pay it all back," Mona said tearfully. "I promise."

"We could have a Fire Fund, Mrs. Matz," I said, "and reimburse you within a reasonable length of time. How about it?"

"Oh, all right. It isn't as if the entire motel burned down."

"It really isn't very serious," I said. "It could have been, but it isn't."

"Still, the principle of the thing—"

"Of course."

Mrs. Matz sat down on the bed and sighed. "Why not the Uptown? Oh, why not the Uptown?"

"Let's discuss the details in the office," I suggested, taking her arm and swooping her out the door. I don't believe she has noticed the severed TV cords yet.

VIII

Tuesday, November 6

Here in Pineville, Idaho, the Ford Pickup Capital of the World, I find myself with a G.E. toaster selling Pop Tarts at school for twenty-five cents each.

We call it the Fire Fund when asked, and so far the principal thinks the counselor approved it, and vice versa.

Over the weekend I mentioned to Angel that it would be nice to have a toaster in town, and she walked over to the cupboard and handed me one.

Jordy said he needed a string of Christmas lights and an extension cord for a project, which she promptly found.

"Anything else?" she asked.

"That should do it," I said. I already had a transistor radio.

On Monday each Bear Flatter donated twenty dollars for the Pop Tarts, to be refunded with interest at the conclusion of the project.

"It's pure junk food," Netty complained as we filled up a cart in Food King.

"Anything for the Fund," I said.

Next we went to the Super Seven, and then to the Corner Grocery. We bought every package of Pop Tarts in Pineville.

"I don't feel good spending $140 for Pop Tarts," Jordy complained. "That's food for a month.

"Can't we start small," he continued, "say ten boxes to begin with? Then if the project is successful, we come back uptown each night and buy more. What will we do with 840 Pop Tarts if they don't sell? Especially since you won't let us eat them?"

"If we are successful on Tuesday, Jordy," I explained, "on Wednesday there will be a dozen other dudes selling Pop Tarts, from their lockers, just like us.

"But if there are no Pop Tarts to be purchased in Pineville, there will be no competition on Wednesday or Thursday—"

"Or Friday—" Jordy nodded.

We went back over to school to set up for today. Lots of other kids were there because of school play rehearsal in the auditorium—Joe Grant, Mike Harvey, and Budd Swaney. Lots of seniors.

We rigged up my locker because there was an electrical outlet just a few feet away, and the other six did not want to do it to theirs. We used theirs for supplies.

We filled that old gray locker of mine with Pop Tarts

boxes, Angel's toaster, and my transistor radio, tuned to country music. On the outside, around the door, we taped a double row of Christmas lights. We taped the extension cord along the wall and plugged it in.

Would you believe, Mrs. C., in the metamorphosis of an old gunmetal gray locker? We all sat down on the floor and admired it.

Several cute girls stopped to ask what we were doing.

"The Fire Fund," I answered.

"Oh, yes," Alicia Akerlow exclaimed. "We wanted to join, but it was the same month as the school play."

"Too bad," Mona said. "You can donate, however, and that's participating in a sense. It starts tomorrow morning."

"We will," Alicia said. "We'll tell all the kids in the play."

We sat for a long time watching the flickering lights and listening to the music. We could have sat there all night, I suppose, feeling good, but we did have homework.

"Our financial endeavors must not interfere with our scholarship," I reminded the others. "Time to head home."

"Yes, master," they all said.

Just then Mr. Taylor, the drama coach, came down the hall for a drink of water.

"What are you students doing here?" he asked, looking curiously at my locker.

"The Fire Fund, Mr. Taylor," Martin said.

Mr. Taylor hesitated. "Fire Fund," he said. "A worthy project. Hope it will be as successful as last year."

He leaned over for a drink. When he turned to go he said, "Why don't you write it up for the school paper? Turn it in to Mrs. Christensen. She would appreciate it, I'm sure."

"Thanks," I said. "I will."

And although it wasn't quite what he had in mind, Mrs. C., I just did.

Wednesday, November 7

I believe we could have sold all 840 Pop Tarts in one morning, except the bell rang and I had to close my locker. Angel's good old toaster could not pop up fast enough. And the scarcity increased the demand.

As I rushed down the hall after first period, I saw the principal, Mr. Fitzhugh, standing in front of my locker. He frowned, then smiled and tapped his foot to the music, then frowned again. He moved around the corner just before the rush.

Mona and I stayed after school for play practice business. I guess she felt obligated—which she should— but she is a real pro with a toaster.

As soon as we turned on the radio, we had business. Joe Grant and Budd Swaney came prowling out of the auditorium toward us.

Joe Grant called, "I'll take half a dozen of whatever you are selling."

"A dollar fifty and you've got it," I said.

Mona already had two Pop Tarts coming out of the toaster.

Budd Swaney stood with his thumbs hooked in the

front pockets of his baggy white pants, looking down his nose at us. "A freshman project?" he sneered.

"Knock it off," Joe said. "Your one-liner in the play is no senior undertaking."

Old Swaney pouted and moved over to the fountain for a drink.

Joe piled the Pop Tarts on top of his English literature book. (Sorry, Mrs. C.) "Thanks, Callahan," he said. "Very enterprising."

He jerked his head at Budd Swaney. "Come on, Swaney," he said.

A new adjective for old Jake here is *enterprising*. Enterprising J. R. Callahan. J. R. C., the enterpriser. A good piece of language, Mrs. Christensen.

Thursday, November 8

All day long kids look at me—differently—as if I am a new student. "Hey," they say, "aren't you the dude who sells Pop Tarts?"

Mike Harvey asked bluntly, "Who's your wholesale source? I can't find those things anywhere in town."

Jinny Thornwall, in living color, whispered across the aisle in English, "I like your lights."

Friday, November 9

I guess it would be safe to say that the Fire Fund was equally as successful as, if not more successful than, last year.

For a while I was right up there with popular. Then we reached our goal. And I was tired of burning my fingers on frosting. Also what would Angel think if she read *Pop Tart King* under my senior class picture?

But it was a great gimmick. And the glow lingers on.

Monday, November 12

Mrs. Matz almost keeled over on her green grasshoppers when we handed her the money—$150 in small change. I don't think she had expected it at all. She shook my hand for almost fifteen minutes.

Then Dumb Mona decided to thank me. She threw her arms around my neck and almost squeezed the breath out of me.

After, at Mrs. Matz's suggestion, we all sat around the office and ate junk food and watched TV and "laughed our heads off" (a hyperbole, Mrs. C., that my dad, George F. Callahan, uses).

What I really need to get ahead in Pineville, Idaho, is a Ford pickup truck. A Ford pickup, a G.E. toaster— what's the difference?

IX

Friday, November 16

Bear Flats mothers are naturally uninhibited, Mrs. Christensen, but if I told you how they bragged when all seven of us made the honor roll first quarter . . .

Would you believe five mothers in cowboy hats walking arm in arm down Big Bear Canyon to meet the school bus? During a November snowfall?

Mr. Bernelli didn't. He thought they were a herd of deer. He slammed on the brakes and opened the door to yell at them. And they hopped right on the bus.

They all talked at once. They hugged their own and everyone else's, and one kept hugging Mr. Bernelli. (Mrs. Davis is a lot like Drift.) But no one was embarrassed, except perhaps Mr. Bernelli, who is not a Bear Flatter.

Then Mrs. Robbins announced that she had a little treat for us. She did not have to tell us what it was:

her all-time, all-American, homemade raisin-filled cookies, still warm from the oven. (I wonder if she could teach Mona the Short or Netty the Tall to make those on a hot plate?)

Anyway, we all ate raisin-filled cookies, and congratulated ourselves.

Angel was "walking on cloud nine," as my dad would say. Also tickled pink and pleased as punch. Just before she floated off the bus at our stop, she reached over to Mr. Bernelli and patted him on the head.

"You must be a very proud bus driver," she said. "Very proud indeed."

Monday, November 19

Cold roast. And hot scalloped potatoes. Mrs. Matz brought over the potatoes from her own oven. (Jordy gets it so easy.)

Now that Motel Management is somewhat under control, I hope to direct more energy to Popularity at School. Had I known it depended upon electrical gimmicks, I would have rigged up my locker long ago.

Flash!

I was sitting here in bed in my warm flannel pajamas made by Angel thinking I was through writing in my journal for the night, when something worth noting happened: Mrs. Matz paid a visit.

She stood outside the door and called, "Let me in, Little Cold Lambs. Let me in."

She could not knock, I found out after I opened the door, because her arms were piled high with quilts.

"Warm quilts for little lambs far from home," she sang.

Now I have seen Angel flying through the house in her old pink bathrobe with her long gray hair hanging down her back. And she looks like a gray-haired angel in a pink bathrobe.

But Mrs. Matz, downstage center, in her multicolored bathrobe was something else.

Her bathrobe was held together with yellow duck safety pins. The pockets hung down from the bottom seams with things that should be in the pockets pinned on with more yellow duck safety pins: handkerchiefs, letters, cough drop boxes, elastic bands, and reading glasses.

Perched on her head were her regular green plastic grasshoppers, exposed to the world without cover of the warbonnet. On her feet were fuzzy brown house slippers with plastic eyes on each side that rolled when she walked—like dark things expiring.

She was an amazing sight, Mrs. C., one that I hope never to see again in my bedroom.

She danced around our room, talking sometimes to us and sometimes to Mr. Matz, who has been gone for ten years.

"It's thirty-two degrees," she said gleefully. "Mrs. Matz's quilt weather. I knew it before I turned on the TV. I'll never get warm tonight, even with the heating pad on high. Oh, Carter, I miss your big warm feet."

She spread two mammoth quilts over Martin and Drift, and two over Jordy and me.

"I'd like to say a thing or two to the builder who built this cardboard motel," she said. "No insulation. Just like I told you, Carter, when we bought it. No insulation."

I suppose if she could talk to her husband, she might as well talk to the builder, too.

She tucked in the quilts at the bottoms of our beds—would you believe, Mrs. C.?—calling each one by name. Lone Star, Flying Geese, Log Cabin, and Distelfink.

"Distelfink?" Drift rolled his eyes.

"Ah, yes, the distelfink bird," she said smiling. "One of my favorites. A Pennsylvania Dutch bird, to watch over you.

"Little Lambs," she said breathlessly, "these are not ordinary motel blankets. These are heirloom quilts Mrs. Matz pieced and quilted herself to cover her own little lambs—bless their hearts—who have grown up and gone away.

"But Mrs. Matz still knows that when the temperature drops to thirty-two, it's time to get her warm quilts out of her cedar chest."

She stood between our beds, smiling down at us. "How do you feel now?"

"Warm, " I gasped, sinking down. I could hardly breathe with all that batting on top of me.

"I think I have a fever," Drift said.

"Could the girls use a couple of these?" Martin suggested.

"I have already taken some to the girls," she said. "Wedding Rings and Bethlehem Stars and Irish Chains. Girls get even colder than boys. Of course"—she moved over to the north wall and felt it—"I should not have put you boys in this end room. This north wall is cold all year. Would you like to move to another room?"

"Right this minute?" Jordy asked. "In the middle of the night?"

"We like to think we are protecting the girls from the north wind," Martin said.

"I thought there was some reason I put you here," Mrs. Matz said. "Now, if you need more quilts, let me know. And don't wait until morning. Call me on the telephone. Any hour of the night. I don't want anyone catching cold in my motel."

"Thanks very much, Mrs. Matz," I said, "and don't worry about our getting cold in the night. I would say it's practically impossible."

"Our mothers made us flannel pajamas," Jordy said, "with our initials on the pockets."

I kicked him under the covers.

"Did you save any quilts for yourself?" I quickly added.

"A cedar chest full," Mrs. Matz said, waving her multicolored arms. "Good night, Little Warm Lambs."

"Good night, Mrs. Matz."

Tuesday, November 20

It isn't Jinny Thornwall in English who likes me. It's Rita Judd in U.S. history.

Rita Judd walked up to me today with her shining black hair and flashing black eyes and said, "Aren't you the dude who sells Pop Tarts at his locker?"

I said, "Sure." I began to melt on the spot. The

combination of shining black hair and black eyes does that to me.

"Meet me after school," she said.

I caught my breath. "I'm sorry, I am not selling them any more," I said. "We reached our goal."

"That's all right. Meet me anyway."

"Why?"

"Aren't you the dude who lives at the Scenic-Vu Motel?"

"Sure."

"Well, I'll walk you home—to the motel."

I said okay because what else could I say? My experience with girls is limited to pounding on their walls.

"Don't wait for me tonight," I told Jordy between classes.

"Why not?"

"I sort of have a date with a girl."

"What do you mean 'sort of'?"

"She's walking me home."

"Wow!"

"I'll say wow!"

"Who is it?"

"Rita Judd."

"I'll say wow again!"

"Keep it quiet, will you, Jordy? And I'll tell you all about it later."

"Sure, Jake. Keep cool."

After school I sauntered down to the front door, six feet tall in my cowboy boots. (Just for the record.) Rita Judd, in living color, was leaning against the wall waiting for me. She was one gorgeous girl in tight Levi's, boots, and a pink parka.

"Where's your pickup?" she asked, bouncing over to my side.

I should have known it was too easy.

I gulped. "I thought we were walking." I slung my backpack over my shoulder.

She laughed and her black eyes really started to sparkle. "This time."

We walked down the front steps together and headed across the lawn like everyone else. Frozen grass doesn't do much for conversation, and I was glad when we reached the sidewalk. All those wrinkled leaves were now crackling and snapping to beat the band, right under our boots.

"Nice sound isn't it?" I said.

"What?"

"The leaves."

"Leaves?" She wrinkled her nose. "You're crazy."

Oh, well—

"We have free bus service to school," I said. "Saves on gas."

"You worried about gas?"

"My mom worries about everything." (Good old Angel.)

"Oh, well, you have a motel room."

"Yes, thanks to the board of education."

"Lucky you."

"I guess so."

"Why, you have lots of rules?"

"No. Just two."

"What are they?"

"The rules?"

She nodded.

"Oh, just a couple of rules we voted on. Sort of like club rules, you know." I did not feel like telling a complete stranger—not even Rita Judd in living color—our personal rules.

"So what are they?"

"Oh, just—Study Hard and Have Fun," I said quickly. (I wonder if anyone can get anything out of me?)

"All—right," she drawled.

X

Wednesday, November 21

In history I asked Rita Judd if I could walk her home
after school. She said not five miles! She said she waits
at the medical clinic for her mother to get off work. I
said I would walk her to the clinic, but she said no,
she would walk me home.

Then I remembered I would have to walk fast to
catch the bus at the motel because tomorrow is
Thanksgiving. How could I forget Thanksgiving? Only
Rita Judd could make me forget Thanksgiving.

I told her she could walk me home next Monday.

Mrs. Matz wished us all a very happy Turkey Day
and said she would miss us like the dickens.

Monday, November 26

Did I ever OD on turkey, Mrs. Christensen.

Everyone in Bear Flats got together at the church and, as my dad would say, "ate their heads off." My dad also shouted patriotic tributes from time to time, beginning almost every sentence with *irregardless*.

I told Dad it was a nonword. He said how could it be when it was such a good one?

Angel was almost her old self again, although she is still worried about the motel, and the Russians coming across the Strait.

Thanksgiving was great, but it was also nice to get back to the good old Scenic-Vu.

Mrs. Matz met us at the bus. "Welcome home," she said, holding out her arms. "Let me help you. Let me carry the cold roast."

"It's turkey," Jordy said, handing her the plastic container.

"Turkey needs to get right in the refrigerator," she said. She followed us Males into our room and sat down on Martin and Drift's bed with the turkey.

"I have never known a weekend so long," she said. "Not a soul—that is, nobody I want to count stayed here all weekend. Thanksgiving weekend and one traveling salesman puffing a cigar, stinking up the entire motel. I put him in Room 2, but next time—"

"Out in the parking lot on his head," Drift interjected.

"That's exactly what I will do," Mrs. Matz continued, "because I have young people here now. Young people still growing. Imagine that cigar smoke filtering into my quilts and pillows, stunting your growth."

She jumped up and put the turkey in the refrigerator. "No milk," she exclaimed. "If you want a glass of milk before you go to school, you know who has a big white refrigerator full."

We were hurrying around the room, hanging up clothes and collecting our books.

"And I think I will have a neon sign installed under my regular sign: No Vacancy to Cigar Smokers.

"Sunday night," she continued, "last night, a nice older couple stopped in, and I suppose I should count them although the weekend was about over. They were just too tired to drive the rest of the way home.

"They had been to their daughter's in Jackson Hole for Thanksgiving. The roads were wet and dark, and it's hard for older people to drive at night, especially if they wear glasses."

"Oh?" Jordy said.

"Glare," Mrs. Matz explained. "And both of them wore glasses, I noticed. Hers were very much out of style—pointed plastic rims. They were no doubt an old pair she had in the car for driving. Though when they pulled up, her husband was driving. I noticed that. I always notice who is driving. Got that habit from my husband. How I miss him, the love.

"They're still here, sleeping in, so whisper as you go past Room 4. I put them in 4 so it would be quiet on both sides."

"Now I know why you put us in 9," Martin said.

Mrs. Matz chatted on. "I know you are in a hurry

to get to school on a Monday morning. Mr. Bernelli cuts it too close. What can I do to help you? Can you make me a quick shopping list? I'll get your groceries from Food King.

"Then after school you can just stay home and relax and study. Those high school teachers give too much homework. Guess they can't remember how it was to be young. They are all as old as the hills. Just like the board of education."

"About the shopping, Mrs. Matz," I said, heading out the door, "that's taking advantage. Our folks would not like it. But thanks, anyway."

"Yes, I understand," she said. "But I would like to. So run along to school now. Here come the girls. And remember to hurry home. I'm glad I'm not as old as those high school teachers."

(She said it, Mrs. Christensen. I didn't.)

"And when you pass the office," she went on, "take a peek inside. I set up my quilting frames over the weekend, and I have a quilt on. I always set up at Thanksgiving and take down at Easter. Thanksgiving to Easter I quilt. I piece during the warm months, when business is better."

"We'll be late if we do," Mona called. "We'll stop in after school. See you, Mrs. Matz."

November 26 was a cold, cold day and we ran to keep warm. I like the feeling of warm running through cold. I like the sound of boots thumping on the hard sidewalk. It was a good cold day to be living.

I wondered how long it would take Mrs. Matz to finish a quilt and how much room it took up in the office. I was planning to invite Rita Judd in for hot chocolate and a little TV.

Rita Judd sat in history, just as gorgeous as I remembered.

"Want to run home?" I asked.

"Why run?"

"It makes a great sound on the sidewalk, and it's too cold to walk."

"You're crazy," she said.

We walked all the way home. Girls do not run, she told me.

I was about to say some were running with me this morning, but I didn't want to say anything to lose Rita Judd. Girls can be eccentric, I know. But I thought they all ran.

Rita was shivering, so I asked her to come into the office for some hot chocolate. I was planning to ask her in *irregardless* of the weather.

She said not in an office, and took off down Main for the clinic.

I started after her, but she called out, "See you later. Okay?"

I called, "Okay."

I went inside, shivering myself.

All the other Bear Flatters were standing in the narrow space between the door and the registration counter. Beyond that, covering the length and width of the room, was Mrs. Matz's quilt, spread out on wooden frames that were tied at each corner to chair backs.

"It's a Motel Special," Mrs. Matz called cheerily, leaning over the mammoth thing with needle and yarn in hand.

"Just a few more minutes and then you can help me roll it a couple of rolls. Then you can sit down here on the sofa as usual." She was obviously proud of her setup.

"A Motel Special?" Helen asked. She held Ralphy up for a bird's-eye view.

"A Motel Special"—Mrs. Matz chuckled—"is made from all the clothes my guests leave in their rooms: men's pants, women's pantsuits, jackets, bathrobes, bathrobes, and bathrobes. I tie a quilt like this once a year—it's too bulky to quilt—and then I start my patchwork quilts.

"One year I pieced a quilt entirely from silk neckties left hanging over chairs. Now why, I ask you, would a salesman who arrived in a suit and tie leave his tie behind?"

We shook our heads, speechless.

"It isn't crowded in here, it's cozy," she continued. "And it never bothers the few customers who stop here during the winter months. Sometimes when I'm busy quilting, I wish they would just keep driving."

"Where's the telephone?" Mona asked suddenly.

"I put the telephone down here on the floor beside me and the TV on the counter where the postcard stand was."

"What did you do with the postcards?" Drift demanded.

"Under the quilt." Mrs. Matz motioned with her

head. "If anyone wants a postcard, he can crawl under the quilt or come back in the spring.

"Still, he would be thankful he came to the Scenic-Vu instead of the Uptown that Mr. Angus Webb thinks is uptown. I don't call six blocks east of Food King uptown. I call that out of town.

"I told that to Mr. Angus Webb one day, and he said names don't matter. He said regardless of the name, he gets them going west and I get them going east.

"I told him that's on the first trip through town. The next time I get them going east and west.

"Now, if one of you will help me roll, there will be room for all of you to sit down on the sofa."

"Males and Females together," Martin asked, "on the same sofa?"

"On second thought . . ." Mrs. Matz bristled. "Now understand, all of you, the quilt does not change a thing in this office. Same old rules."

"Same old rules," we echoed.

Because of the quilt, we almost forgot to go to Food King. It was snowing to beat the band when we walked uptown, and coming back we collected about two inches of snow on top of our groceries.

After supper we went back to the office.

About seven o'clock a salesman came in. He paused in the doorway, looking around.

"Anybody home?"

"We are all here," Mrs. Matz said, looking up from the quilt.

"This *is* a motel?"

"You read the sign, didn't you—the Scenic-Vu Motel? You stopped, didn't you?"

"Well"—he brushed snow from his shoulders—"if this is a Senior Sneak, I don't want to stay here."

"This is no Senior Sneak," Mrs. Matz said. "I can tell you that. Do you need a postcard?"

"I need a room," the man said impatiently.

"Put your twenty dollars on the counter and you've got one," Mrs. Matz said. "Room 2." She began quilting again. "It's large with a view, though this time of night you won't open your draperies for the view, so take five dollars off the counter. Catch!"

She reached into her pocket for a key and tossed it across the quilt to the man. It hit the counter with a loud clink.

The man was trying to make change, catch the key, and keep an eye on us all at the same time. It was almost too much for him.

"You sure this isn't a school basketball team?" he asked.

"Guess again," Helen piped up from the sofa.

"You wouldn't believe it if she told you," Drift added. "Don't worry about it."

Mrs. Matz smiled pleasantly at the man. "Let me know if there is anything you want, though I don't suppose there will be. Don't ask for a postcard, however."

"Why not?"

"This is not the time of year to be sending postcards," Mrs. Matz explained. "There is some nice stationery in the dresser drawer in your room—three

74

sheets and an envelope under the Gideons' Bible. So write a letter if you want. Same difference—long postcard with scribbling up the side or a short letter. What's your name?"

"Uh—uh—Milton Moser," he mumbled. "And I don't need a postcard." He hurried out with the key.

"Milton Moser, my foot," Netty said. "I hope he forgets his necktie."

It was nice in the office tonight, sitting around that big Motel Special, feeling warm and secure and proud and independent all at the same time.

Now I am sounding poetic like Jordy, not like Jake. Maybe it's Mrs. Matz's quilt. Oh, gosh, maybe it's love. Maybe I'm in love with Rita Judd.

XI

Tuesday, November 27

Mrs. Christensen, you could be no more surprised than I was when I found out the last entry last night was not the last event of the night. Talk about Chaucer's "Knight's Tale"—you want to hear mine?

A loud knock on the door wakened me from a sound sleep.

I grabbed the bedspread and wrapped it around me and ran to the door. "Mrs. Matz?" I called, switching on the light.

"It's me." Someone giggled. "Open up. I'm freezing."

I opened the door an inch and peered out. It was Rita Judd, in living color, and another gorgeous girl.

"Surprise," Rita said. "Let us in."

"It's after midnight—"

"The perfect time for a party!"

"I'm not dressed—"

"All—right!" They pushed against the door and they were inside. "Shut the door. We're freezing."

I shut the door.

"This is Annabel," Rita said.

"Annabel who?" I asked weakly.

"Annabel Sanders."

"Hi," I whispered. "We can't have any girls in our room."

Rita moved over close to me. In fact, she stood on the bedspread. "We are not *any* girls," she said. She tossed her shiny black hair. "Now get rid of a couple of those."

Martin, Drift, and Jordy were sitting straight up in bed with expressions of sheer horror on their faces. Martin was reaching for his hat.

"They live here too," I whispered. "They're in bed."

"I know, stupid."

Annabel set down two six-packs of beer on the floor, leaned back against the door, and switched off the light.

Oh, madness! Trying to reach the bed lamp, I stumbled over the stupid bedspread and knocked the lamp shade off.

Jordy turned it on.

"You can't stay, Rita," I said, collapsing on the end of the bed. "Why did you come here this time of night? What do you have there?"

"I know." Drift raised his hand. "It's booze. And some of us are only fourteen. It will have to go. Sorry."

"No," Martin said, "the beer stays and the girls go."

Drift shook his head. "No, the girls stay, and the beer goes."

"Shut up," I muttered. I tied a bulky knot in the bedspread and held out my arms in exasperation.

"Rita, can you understand that we have this real strict landlady—" Unconsciously I began rubbing my head.

The other boys rubbed their heads, except Martin, who had his hat on.

"We are under board of education rules," Jordy squeaked.

"How did you get here, anyway?" I asked.

"Stole my old man's pickup." Rita laughed. "Clever, don't you think?"

"Practice makes perfect," Annabel said.

They both giggled. And sat down on the floor.

"Rita—" I faltered. "We could go to the office—we could watch the late late movie." I would do almost anything for Rita Judd.

"Go to the office to booze up and make out? My old man knows Mrs. Matz. He'd kill me."

"But it's okay in this room?"

"Stupid, he wouldn't know." She nodded to Annabel. "Let's split!"

Annabel rolled her eyes and then focused on my pajama pocket. "J.R.C.," she sneered. "You picked a real winner this time, Rita."

I grabbed Rita's hand. She lurched away. I moved to the door fast and held it shut.

"I'm sorry," I said. "Let's go talk in your pickup. In private. Please?"

She said nothing.

I was losing Rita Judd. I could not lose Rita Judd.

"To heck with the rules," I said in desperation. "You are both cordially invited to stay in this motel room. For you, Rita Judd, and you, Annabel Sanders, we will break all rules. Sit down, and let's start this late late conversation all over again."

I grabbed two chairs from the kitchenette and offered them. "Second chance?"

"All right. All right. I reconsider. Second chance," Rita said.

We all laughed. Then there was a long silence.

"So," I said, tightening the knot in the bedspread, "what should we talk about? U.S. history?"

No one laughed.

I offered the chairs again.

Rita and Annabel took off their parkas and tossed them on the chairs. They dropped down on my bed and sat cross-legged. With their boots on.

"Help!" Jordy moaned. He slid down his pillow and disappeared under the covers.

"What's the matter now?" Rita asked.

"Oh, it's nothing," I stammered. "It's just Mrs. Matz. She is really fussy about her Flying Geese and—"

"Her geese?"

I nodded. "And her Distelfink."

"And her distelfink?"

"And over here—" Martin was waving his arms over the quilts—"we have her Log Cabin and her Lone Star." He tipped his cowboy hat at the end of his speech.

There was another long silence.

"It doesn't get any better," Rita said. She frowned at Annabel.

"Should we try the pickup?" I asked again.

The girls jumped up and grabbed their parkas from the chairs.

"Do you want to know what I think?" Annabel said to Rita. She zipped up her parka fast. "I think they are all nuts. That's what I think."

"Why didn't you say you were straight?" Rita sneered at me.

"Why would I need to?"

She picked up the six-packs and gave me a look of scorn that I will never forget.

For a long time after they left, I sat on the side of the bed, staring at the distelfink birds in the quilt. Wanting to die.

"We have been hoping and praying for girls to break in here all fall, and we let them get away," Drift muttered.

"Did someone let those gorgeous girls get away?" Jordy asked.

"I love girls who bring booze to our room in the middle of the night," Martin said. "Tell me it wasn't a dream."

They were just talking, trying to make me feel better. I will never feel better.

Wednesday, November 28

I smiled at Rita in U.S. history. I waved. She did not even look my way.

Hard as it is for me to admit, Rita Judd does not like me, Jacob R. Callahan, as a person. I think maybe she needed something to write in her senior journal.

Thursday, November 29

When I was wakened again last night by knocking on the door, I thought, in my stupor, that maybe I was getting another chance. How lucky can a guy get?

The knocks came fast—crack, crack, crack—like a dozen gorgeous girls knocking at once.

I pulled on my Levi's and rushed to the door. Rita Judd and all her girl friends could come into my motel room and drink beer all night if Rita would just smile on me again.

(Gosh, can anyone make me do anything?)

I reached for the doorknob and then stopped. I heard girls giggling, and then Rita Judd call, "Open the door, Jake. I'm freezing."

I did not open the door. (I don't always do *anything*.)

The knocking came again, faster. Crack, crack. I wonder how I knew it was eggs, having never been egged before?

I went back to bed and stared at the stupid distelfink birds. They might as well be black crows.

As in everything else, Mrs. C., there is a great difference in girls.

Friday, November 30

Riding home to Bear Flats tonight I got to wondering—what's the purpose?

What's the purpose of all those elements I am told to memorize in chemistry—Fe, Mg, and C. Mr. Van Wagoner nearly scared the wits out of me today when he said everything in the world was on that periodic table in front of me—pickups, motels, universities, even me!

Is high school so important that I live in a motel for it? So I can go to the university and live in a dormitory? So I can become a chemist and go back to Bear Flats and plant a garden?

My dad did it all—university diploma and job with G.E. After a while he thought, What's the use? And he went up to Bear Flats and started planting.

I don't know if Angel gave up or not. It's hard to know about your own mother. Sometimes I think she did. Sometimes I think she didn't.

She was an English major who read a thousand books. She is the one who tells me about *irregardless*. I asked her why she doesn't tell Dad. She said she has been telling him for twenty years.

So what's the use?

If I had a pickup, I would drive back to town tonight and five miles farther to see Rita Judd.

Also, why do I care if I am on the honor roll at Pine Valley High School? And if I don't know that, why am I insisting that all the Bear Flatters be on it?

And by the way, Mrs. C., what is the real purpose of this journal:

To develop the right side of my brain?

To introduce myself to me?

To improve my use of the beloved language?

Or is it just a needless requirement to get me out of Pine Valley High School, out of the hair of the board of education? I hand over a journal, and they hand me a diploma?

When you read this, Mrs. C., if you ever do, please send the answer. You can send it to the Scenic-Vu Motel. Mrs. Matz will forward it.

XII

Monday, December 3

You keep asking, Mrs. Christensen, how am I coming
with my magnum opus? Oh, gosh, Mrs. C., what you
expect and what you receive may not be one and the
same. And whatever is a magnum opus anyway?

Please graduate me, Mrs. C., *irregardless*.

Angel says I am preparing myself for my future,
one step at a time. She says the view from the bottom
step is not all that great, but that I should not get
discouraged.

I said to her, "Don't you feel trapped up here in
Bear Flats, picking peas and feeding chickens? With
no library?"

She said, "No place is perfect. I like Bear Flats for
what it is. Your dad is happy here and that's one reason

84

I like it. There are no poisons in those peas or those chickens, and that's another reason.

"And I think maybe I've read too many books. How do you think I know what to worry about?"

She had a point there.

"I think you are the one who feels trapped, Jake," she said. "And that is perfectly normal. You need to educate yourself, prepare yourself, and find your own place in life."

"You kicking me out, Angel?" I asked.

"No. You're pushing. If I did the planning, we would still be out in the hammock, singing and playing the guitar. Remember?"

So here I am at the Scenic-Vu Motel on step two, you might say. Looking for the view. And to be honest, the view from this step is no Paradise Island.

But I'll keep looking. I'll keep hoping. And one of these days I will look out and I will see the promised view.

And it had better be good!

Tuesday, December 4

Town girls have beautiful names:

> Jinny Thornwall
> Amber Attwood
> Cindy Hayes
> Lisa Lillywhite
> Jinny Thornwall

If it sounds as if I am only interested in girls and food, that's only partially true, Mrs. C. School is very important to me and I attend regularly every day from eight until three. Following are my classes and teachers:

Psychology	Miss Millet
English	Mrs. Christensen!!
Math	Mr. Houser
Chemistry	Mr. Van Wagoner
U.S. History	Mr. Sullivan
Auto Mechanics	Mr. Abel
P.E.	Coach Cottino

School is the same, day after day. (I didn't say English is boring, Mrs. C. I just said it is English every day.)

And I don't know about that Chaucer guy. He may have really been something in his day—but today?

Also, you keep saying "Apply, Apply," just like my dad says "Show initiative, Show initiative."

I'm trying, Mrs. C., I'm trying. For example, take that Greek you have been trying to teach us.

According to what you say—the Pineville students of Pine Valley High School are Pinevillophiles and Bear Flatophobes because they think they are cool and we are not, whereas we are Bear Flatophiles and Pinevillophobes for opposite reasons.

I'm applying, Mrs. C., I'm applying.

Wednesday, December 5

I am still tutoring in the office every night. I've threat-
ened the Bear Flatters with no food at all if they don't
stay on the honor roll.

Staying on the honor roll is more important to me
than girls or food. Now, that is down in writing.

After school today we Bear Flatters were running
down good old Elm Street as hard and loud as we could,
when I felt an impulse to call roll.

"Stop!" I yelled.

Everyone came to a grinding halt, piling up on each
other. All breathless like a pack of wild animals.

"Anybody left behind in the girls' room?" I asked,
looking around. "One—two—three—four—"

"Don't look at me," Drift said breathlessly. "I don't
even go near that radiator—"

"Four Dudes. One—two—three Dudettes," I counted.
"That makes seven Bear Flatters." I was short-winded
myself.

"So?" Mona yelled, hopping around in a little circle.
Glaring at me.

"So"—I waved my arms around in the air—"so,
Bear Flatters, keep your boots on!"

We all took off again, running through the cold December day.

It's snowing to beat the band now. I can't even see
the cedar tree under the neon sign.

I just bet Martin that this is the only motel in Idaho
with two pictures exactly alike in the same room. They

87

are bolted to the wall above our beds. One is *Fisherman with Trout*, and the other is *Fisherman with Trout*.

Martin says, "Make it the whole world."

Jordy says, "Turn one upside down."

And Drift says, "Trade one with the girls. They may have a couple of *Nudes on Beach*."

Thursday, December 6

Out of the clear blue sky I said to Mrs. Matz, "Do you know anyone in this town who has an old car or truck for sale? An old thing that nobody wants because it uses too much gas and oil? An old clunker I could fix up? Something cheap?"

She looked up from her quilting with a strange smile on her face. "I do," she said.

"You do?"

"I do," she repeated.

"Where?"

"In the garage."

I knew Mrs. Matz had a garage at the end of a long driveway east of the motel, with a nondescript compact car parked in front. I had thought she couldn't lift the garage door.

Now she was telling me there was an old car in there waiting for me, Jake R. Callahan, to change its oil and pump up its tires.

"What kind is it?" I was hoping for an old Chevy or

even an old Jeep. A Ford pickup would be asking for too much.

"Probably a Ford. With that dealership over in Fielding, nearly everyone in Pineville buys a Ford. I haven't driven it for ten years. I almost forgot I had it. Carter bought it when our children were in high school."

"What kind of old Ford?" I asked.

"Blue," she said. "Blue on the bottom, anyway."

"A covered wagon?" Drift asked.

"You mean you haven't driven it for ten years?" I asked. A pile of rusted parts was a bit older than I had in mind.

"I'm afraid not," Mrs. Matz said. "But my children drive it every summer when they come to visit. They tell me to drive it or sell it.

"Of course, that is just what I intend to do every summer. But when it's back in the garage and I don't see it, I forget about it.

"I just hop in my little compact and buzz uptown and parallel park on Main Street easy as pie. And on a thimbleful of gas, too."

The most important question I was almost afraid to ask. "How much?"

"To the gallon? Don't ask me that. Even if I knew once, I don't know now."

"How much *money*?"

"Oh." Mrs. Matz looked around at each one of us. "I haven't the slightest idea. But not much, I can tell you that right now."

"Approximately."

"Maybe approximately two or three hundred dollars. Does that sound fair?"

"Sounds good. Sounds bad," I said. "I want it. I'm broke."

"You want a part-time job?"

"I'll take it. What is it?"

"Anything you can see around here that needs help. Clean it. Paint it. Pick it up. Throw it away. Weed it. Shovel it. Fix it."

"Thanks. I'm hired."

"But it's strictly part-time," Mrs. Matz said. "Just an hour or two when you are finished with lessons on weekdays. Saturdays when you want to stay over. I do not want to be the subject of your next meeting."

"Can you use me?" Martin asked.

"I could use all four boys and the girls, too, but I can't pay all of you. So it will mostly have to be Jake this year because he's the oldest. But you can help him with jobs he can't do alone."

"Like carrying a paint can?" Martin asked.

"Something like that," Mrs. Matz said. "And Martin, next year you will be first on the list."

"Jake will do it all this year, just to spite us," Drift said. "I'm the one who needs the money. I'm the one who's building a shrine."

"No," Mrs. Matz said. "Minimum wages, minimum time. Besides, Drift, weeds keep growing, paint keeps chipping."

I tried not to run too fast or lift the garage door right off its hinges. And knowing Mrs. Matz, I was prepared to be pleased with anything on flat tires.

"Don't expect anything too good," Jordy whispered,

stooping to help me lift the old wooden door. "Then you won't be disappointed."

"I know, Jordy. I know."

The door swung upward out of my grasp, and I looked in at the car, partially covered with old quilts. Even under the quilts I knew that car. A Ford Thunderbird convertible! About a 1970.

I lifted the quilts slowly, unable to believe my eyes.

Everyone walked around the car admiring it, saying wow.

Mrs. Matz rattled on. "Oh, it was too embarrassing for an old widow to ride around town in a convertible. In this town, anyway.

"For a few years after Carter I used to come out here and sit in it sometimes because it reminded me of him."

She looked at me anxiously. "Is it too old, Jake? Too rusty? Too big and clunky? Tires too flat?"

She tapped the front fender with her thimble still on her third finger.

"It will do," I said, rubbing my hand over the beautiful baby-blue hood. "It will do."

XIII

Friday, December 7

I stayed in Pineville tonight because I wanted to work
on my car. And my new job.

"What will Dad say?" Jordy asked, smashing our
dirty clothes into a grocery sack.

"He will wave his arms around and shout," I said,
"and then he will say, 'Now that's what I call initiative.' "

"Somehow that doesn't sound like what he'll say,"
Jordy said, heading out the door for the bus. ·

"Wait and see," I said. "After he waves and shouts
for a while, Angel will tell him what to say." (Good
old Angel.)

I knew what Angel would tell me also—work before
play—so as soon as the bus left I dashed over to the
office and told Mrs. Matz I was reporting for work.

She said to report back tomorrow, and that there was an electric heater in the garage. (Good old Mrs. Matz.)

I did not expect the car to start, and sure enough, it didn't. But I was not disappointed. I have always dreamed of a car that needed a little fixing up in an old garage.

First thing, I checked the battery. It was good and dead. I took it out and carried it up to Steve's Garage, a block east on Main.

"It just needs recharging," I told Steve. "I'll pick it up tomorrow."

"You bet," he said. "Mrs. Matz's Thunderbird giving her trouble?"

"It needs some work," I said. "I'm buying it. Guess I'll be rolling flat tires up here all night."

Steve nodded pleasantly as he unscrewed the battery cap. "I've been pumping up its tires and changing its oil for ten years," he said. "Love that Thunderbird."

I sauntered over to the oil rack. "What's your best oil, Steve?" (Gosh, was that Jake R. Callahan talking?)

It was late when Mrs. Matz came out to the garage with a flashlight. "Where are you?" she called.

I was sitting behind the steering wheel with my arms spread out over the top of the seat. Smiling like Henry Ford.

"I'm here working on the steering wheel," I answered.

She beamed the flashlight in my face. "Are you going to sleep in here? It's past midnight."

I am in bed now, but I can't sleep. I may never sleep again. I may never lead a normal life again.

Watch out, Pineville, Idaho. Jacob R. Callahan has a car!

Saturday, December 8

My job today was to move the furniture out of Room 1 into Mrs. Matz's porch in preparation for a complete refurbishment. I got it all out except for the bed and the refrigerator. Jordy can help me with those.

After three hours Mrs. Matz said, "That's all for today."

I headed straight for the garage. My car was still there.

I love garages, Mrs. Christensen. I could putter around in one forever, smelling the grease and gas and rubber and leather and wax. And anything else that happens to be there.

I love engines, too, especially the one I was looking at under the hood of my car. All that raw horsepower staring up at me.

I checked the oil, and just as I expected, it was brown as mud. I ran up to Steve's Garage and bought five cans of his best and a new filter, and I changed the oil.

After that I checked the radiator. It was good and low, so I added water.

I ran back up to Steve's for the battery and put it back in.

And then, when I turned the ignition key, that baby-blue car began purring like a kitten.

After the engine was good and warm, I backed the car out of the garage and drove it up and down the driveway a few dozen times, just to get the feel of it. I don't want to drive it anywhere else until it's washed and waxed and looking great.

There are still a dozen other things I must do—drain the radiator, put in antifreeze, lubricate it all over—but I can do those things in auto mechanics. Won't Mr. Abel be surprised when I drive up Monday morning in my own car?

The rest of the day I spent washing and waxing. I was still buffing when Mrs. Matz came with her flashlight again.

"It's twelve o'clock," she said. "Go to bed."

Monday, December 10

What a car!

This morning all the Bear Flatters piled in said car to ride in style to good old Pine Valley High School. Dudes in the front, Dudettes in the back.

Except Mona. She wanted to ride on the front fender, holding on to the hood ornament like a homecoming queen.

I said no to that.

She said if she could not ride on the fender she was riding in the front seat. She hopped in and sat sideways on the Dudes, with her boots sticking up under the steering wheel.

"Punch it!" she said.

I turned on the radio, backed down the driveway, and headed up Main, honking when we passed Steve's Garage, Food King, the Super Seven, the Branding Iron, the Corner Grocery, Al's Drive-In, the Uptown.

Honking most of the time. Singing above the radio. Also shouting, "We've got wheels! We've got wheels!"

"This car rides like a limousine," Mona shouted. "How is it in the back?"

"Ample," Netty called.

Helen leaned up and screeched in my ear that we should go back to the motel for Ralphy and Mrs. Matz because there was *more* than ample room in the backseat.

I said after school, which reminded me . . .

I turned south. We cruised down Juniper (Jinny Thornwall's street) and then we drove up to the auto shop door of Pine Valley High School and honked.

We attracted a great deal of attention, possibly because the top was down—and it was snowing to beat the band.

What a car!

Tuesday, December 11

A grease gun is a marvelous invention. Right up there with grease itself. Today in auto shop I introduced both to my Thunderbird.

At the beginning of school Mr. Sullivan was telling us in U.S. history one of Benjamin Franklin's maxims:

Now that I have a sheep and a cow, everybody bids me good morrow.

Well, now that I have a car . . .

Alicia Akerlow, practically a total stranger, rushed up to me in the hall as if I were her steady and cried, "Oh, Jake, could you drive me home during lunch? I forgot my history notebook. And it's due today. It's right on the kitchen table."

Harvey Broadbent, the student body vice-president, nearly knocked me over with a friendly slap on the back.

"Hey, Callahan," he shouted. "Why didn't you tell us you had a convertible? We could have used it in the homecoming parade for the queen and her attendants to ride in. We asked all around for one. Oh, well, we'll use it another time. Soon!"

Cindy Hayes, one of the smiling Pine Valley High School cheerleaders, waved me down as I was backing out of the shop.

"Jake! Jake!" She poked her head through the open window. "I have a big favor to ask, and I don't know who else to ask. It's that palm tree we used in the assembly—the Welcome Back to School Assembly. You remember. It's really a hall tree underneath and it needs to be returned to Mrs. Boley. She keeps calling. Could you? Since you have a convertible?"

"I just put the top up," I stammered. "There are already seven kids in here—"

"After you drop them off? Could you?"

"Sure." (Can anyone get me to do anything?)

Friday, December 14

I stayed over at the motel again. I went to the basketball game in Fielding with two dudes from auto mechanics, Tom Barlow and John Allen. I drove. Not every teenager in Pineville has a Ford pickup, I'm finding out.

We won 68 to 50.

We cruised Main after. And Juniper. It was a blast.

But a problem I had not anticipated is occurring: gas money.

Saturday, December 15

I put up Christmas lights for Mrs. Matz the complete length of the motel. It took the entire morning, although most of my time was spent untwisting the strings and going up and down the ladder.

Mrs. Matz said it would be worth it, as the lights should attract more business. She has not had any up since her husband died, ten years ago.

She insisted on holding the ladder for me, and every time she talked she jiggled it. I had to watch out for the lights wrapped around my neck and crazy Mrs. Matz, too.

In the afternoon she dragged out of her basement a fully decorated, four-foot-tall Christmas tree, which she set on the counter in the office. Its white boughs sagged with plastic pears and grapes. And garlands of Lifesavers. Pink nylon net encircled the entire thing from the bottom bough to the tinsel star on top.

(Have you ever seen an embalmed Christmas tree, Mrs. Christensen?)

"How do you like it?" Mrs. Matz asked.

"I don't."

"But maybe someone else will," she said. "It takes all kinds, you know."

"It will kill all the business the lights attract," I said.

"Can't be helped," she said cheerily. "I used to have a real tree every Christmas—six feet tall—right over in that corner." She pointed. "But now I quilt. And I won't take down my quilting for anything. Not even Christmas."

Monday, December 17

I washed my car.

This car has changed my personality from insecure to almost aggressive. I asked Jinny Thornwall for a date this Wednesday night, the last day of school before Christmas vacation.

It was easy. She was standing at the front door, loaded down with books, and I said, "Want a ride, Jinny!"

She looked surprised. "I usually drive," she said, "but my mom has the pickup today. Do you have room?"

"Lots," I said. I motioned to the Bear Flatters waiting for me. "They are walking today."

They looked surprised, too. But as I have said be-

fore, they can switch from Dumb to Smart real fast.
They took off across the lawn.

I have been in love with Jinny Thornwall for three
years. And suddenly she was sitting beside me, in
living color, in my own car. I could hardly breathe.

"Where did you get this quaint old car?" she asked.
Her eyes are baby blue, too.

"I'm buying it from my landlady," I answered. "Mrs.
Matz. You know her?"

"Of course I know Mrs. Matz," she said. "Everybody
knows everybody in Pineville."

I drove slowly over to Juniper Street, listening to
her talk. She thinks the journal idea is great, Mrs.
Christensen. Of course, a girl like Jinny would probably have a lot of things to record.

Jinny Thornwall is one beautiful, sincere girl, Mrs.
C. Not a phony cheerleader who smiles *all* the time.
And not fast like Rita Judd! Jinny Thornwall is a real
girl. I don't think I will be able to exist long out of her
company.

I passed her house on Juniper, planning to drive
around the block a few times.

"Stop," she exclaimed. "You passed my house."

I backed up and pulled into her driveway. "I wasn't
thinking about your house," I said.

"What were you thinking about?"

"I was thinking about asking you out this Wednesday. I'm staying over."

She looked out the window. "I don't know," she said.

"Why not?"

"I have never gone out with—"

100

"There's a first time for everything," I said. "How about dinner at the Branding Iron and a movie? Or bowling?"

"Okay," she said, "dinner and a movie."

Lucky me! Only two days until Wednesday!

XIV

Tuesday, December 18

Only one more day until Wednesday!

I washed my car. Snow really gets a car dirty.

I drove uptown for a can of mink oil and got my boots in shape for my big date tomorrow night. (Old six-foot Jake R. Callahan here. Hold your breath, Jinny Thornwall.)

By the time you read this journal, Mrs. C., Jake R. Callahan and Jinny Thornwall may be going steady.

The Christmas lights really did the trick. Mrs. Matz said she has never had so much business the week before Christmas. She turned on the No VACANCY sign for the first time in ten years.

She asked me to drive out to the Uptown to count the cars parked there.

"Only three," I told her. "Three against your seven.

It must be the lights. The Uptown only has them around the office window."

Wish me luck, Mrs. Christensen. I'll make a full report tomorrow night.

Wednesday, December 19

Today is the Day! Be still, O boldly beating heart!

Watch where you are going today, Jake R. Callahan, so you won't walk off a bridge and end up in the hospital instead of at the Gem Theater with Jinny Thornwall.

Why am I writing in this journal before breakfast? *Am* I writing in a journal before breakfast? I wonder what Jinny Thornwall is writing in her journal this morning? I am going crazy because of Jinny Thornwall.

I'll wash my car as soon as I get home from school.

Thursday, December 20

Here is the report, Mrs. Christensen. Or, as my dad would say— But by now you know what my dad would say.

I will make this brief because as I have mentioned before, I do not like to live it and then write it, too.

At seven o'clock I picked up Jinny Thornwall in my newly washed Ford Thunderbird and took her to the Branding Iron for a prime rib dinner.

Everyone was there—Joe Grant, Harvey Broadbent, Cindy Hayes. They all said hi.

It was wonderful sitting in a booth with Jinny, listening to her talk with country music in the background. She loves to talk. I love to listen to her talk.

She likes country music as much as I do. And prime rib. And senior journals! We have a lot in common.

For dessert we had Flaming Cherries Jubilee. Everyone was having Flaming Cherries Jubilee. The place was on fire!

I did not want that meal to end, Mrs. C.

Then we went across the street to the Gem Theater to see good old John Wayne in *Fort Apache*. Everyone was there, too.

Jinny and I stocked up on popcorn and headed down front. We changed seats two or three times because our boots stuck to the floor. Finally we decided the entire floor of the theater was covered with spilled pop, and we settled on row five.

The old black-and-white film kept breaking, but that was part of the fun. Everyone stomped on the floor and applauded when it stopped and when it started again.

And when the Duke himself appeared on the screen in his cavalry uniform, the entire audience cheered loudly. Including Jinny and me.

I did not want the movie to end, either.

But it did, and I had to take Jinny home.

In the car I turned to her and told her how I had not wanted the dinner to end nor the movie to end. I told her I guess that meant I did not want our relationship to end. I said I hoped she would go out with me another time. Maybe after the holidays. Maybe on a Friday night when I stayed over.

104

She looked out of the window past my head and said, "I don't think so."

"You like someone else?"

"No."

"How about giving me a chance then?"

"I don't think so."

"Why not?" I was trying hard to be Cool Jake.

"Just because."

"Just because what?"

"What you said—staying over."

"Staying at the Scenic-Vu? Is that it?"

"Partly."

"Being from Bear Flats?"

"That's the other part."

Old Cool Jake could think of nothing more to say.

She opened the door. "Hey, I don't want to hurt your feelings."

"You didn't."

"See you then. I can walk up alone."

"Sure," I said, smiling at her beautiful town face. "See you around."

"Want to talk?" Mrs. Matz called as I stomped past the office door.

I did not want to talk. I had had enough talk for one night. I slammed the door of Room 9 behind me, kicked off my boots, and flung myself on the bed.

Bear Flats is one problem I cannot solve. It is too big.

XV

Wednesday, January 2

A new year.

And who should I see before school in the library? Jinny Thornwall, in living color, scanning the magazine rack.

I walked over—for auld lang syne—and said hi.

She turned her back on me and began talking to her girlfriend, Amber Attwood. They walked off together, laughing quietly.

Old Jake here went into total depression.

Thursday, January 3

So much for Popularity at School. Now, back to the motel—

*   *   *

I called a meeting in the office to remind everyone that the holidays are over and that the two rules are still in force.

"What were those two rules?" Drift asked. "Can you refresh my memory?"

I ignored the smart aleck. I allotted each person, including Mrs. Matz, five uninterrupted minutes to complain and/or compliment.

I began, "No gas money, no rides to school. No gas money, no rides to Food King. No gas money, no rides to school—"

They all began nodding.

"Also," I said, "I checked with some of your teachers after school today, and two of you are not going to make the honor roll this quarter unless you turn in a book report to Mr. Hudson in English. So the two boys in Mr. Hudson's class can either walk back to the school library right after this meeting or walk over to Mrs. Matz's bookcase in her house."

"Are you through with your five minutes?" Jordy asked.

I nodded.

He turned to Mrs. Matz. "What do you have?"

"Every book required by those old teachers and then some," Mrs. Matz replied. "Remember, all three of my children graduated from Pine Valley High School."

"Drift and I would like to borrow a couple," Jordy said.

Drift was the only one who could talk for five continuous minutes and say nothing—except that he could not remember the rules. Five long minutes and then he signed off by asking for donations for his roadside shrine. What a smart aleck.

The complaints from both the Dudes and the Dudettes were similar:

1. Lengthy showers steaming up the rooms.
2. Lengthy telephone conversations bothering readers.
3. Smelly socks and underclothes scattered around the rooms.
4. No gas money. (My complaint!)

I took care of all the complaints in less than a minute:

1. A ten-minute limit on showers and telephones.
2. A brown paper sack for each person's dirty clothes.
3. A weekly gasoline tax.

Or else!

"Explain the gasoline tax in relation to our two rules, Study Hard and Have Fun," Helen said.

"It's great fun to ride in the car," I explained. "It is not fun to buy the gas out of your lunch money. Any more questions?"

"Do you need any more quilts?" Mrs. Matz asked.

We all agreed we slept semismothered.

"Besides," Jordy added, "all the boys received new flannel pajamas for Christmas with our initials embroidered on the pockets so we won't get them mixed up."

"No compliments?" I asked, looking around. "Meeting adjourned."

*   *   *

It was snowing hard at seven o'clock when the first customer stomped up to the office door. Inside he shook snow all over the place.

"It's no night to be out driving," Mrs. Matz called from across the room, where she sat quilting. She had finished the Motel Special and was now quilting a green-and-white Irish Chain. "But now that you're here you won't need to worry the rest of the night."

"Unless you need a postcard," Netty added. She was quilting next to Mrs. Matz, who was also drilling her on vocabulary words.

"Why?"

"Because the postcard rack is under this quilt," Netty explained, standing up. "However, if you want to crawl under and just take what you grab, you can still put it to use. The picture doesn't really matter anyway."

"I don't need a postcard," the man replied. "Just a room for two—as far from the postcards as possible."

"That will be Room 2," Netty said. She reached into Mrs. Matz's pocket for the key and tossed it to him.

Mrs. Matz was holding her needle in midair, her mouth open.

"It's large with a view," Netty said. "However, this time of night—"

"Room 2? How much?"

"Put twenty dollars on the counter."

"I'll check the room first," the man said, backing out.

Mrs. Matz gulped. "He didn't want a postcard, did he? They usually don't when the rack is in plain sight. They do when it's under the quilt."

"He didn't want one," Netty said.

"Did you tell him about the stationery in the room under the Gideons' Bible? He could spend the entire evening wishing he had a postcard when right there in the drawer are three sheets of stationery with Scenic-Vu Motel printed across the top. We need to tell him that. Looks as if he's getting his luggage out of the trunk."

"He's too tired to write a letter tonight," Mona said, looking out the window. "He can hardly carry his wife's two Gucci suitcases."

"Well, imagine that," Mrs. Matz said, lowering her needle. "You girls are really perceptive. Maybe you should go into the motel business."

The man came back inside and put a twenty-dollar bill on the counter. "Who's in charge here?" he asked, looking puzzled. "If this is a Senior Sneak . . ."

"This is no Senior Sneak," Drift said. "I can tell you that."

Netty walked over to the counter and gave the man four five-dollar bills. "This time of night you won't be able to see the view," she said, "so put five dollars back in your pocket and leave fifteen on the counter."

The man hesitated, but he did as Netty said.

"Also," Netty continued, "don't forget your tie in the morning."

"My tie?"

"Yes, your tie." Netty pointed to her neck. "Some men do, and they never see them again."

Mrs. Matz interjected. "Tell your wife she can come and quilt awhile if she wants to. It's an Irish Chain."

"Oh—I don't think she quilts," the man said. He slowly backed toward the door.

"Well now, don't you make her feel bad over that," Mrs. Matz said. "That's certainly nothing to be ashamed of. We all have to learn sometime. Look at my girls here. They just learned after Thanksgiving and look at them now, taking such tiny stitches you need a magnifying glass to see them."

"This is no Senior Sneak then?" the man mumbled, still backing away.

"I can guarantee that," Mrs. Matz said, smiling. "Now be sure to tell your wife. I don't know many women who don't enjoy a good quilting now and then. Sort of like a good cry. Maybe you don't know every little thing about your wife. Most husbands don't. But do tell her."

"I will, I will," he mumbled. "But she won't, she won't—"

"What I want to know," Drift said, after the man was gone, "is when the seniors do sneak, where do they go?"

"They go to the big town of Fielding and raid the pizza parlor and drive their pickups through the aviary pond," Martin drawled from across the room.

"Pizza?" Drift's face lit up. "Do you think they'd deliver?"

"Shut up, Drift," Martin said. "Here comes another customer."

"It's my turn," Mona said, jumping up from the sofa. She hurried over to the counter and beamed a great big smile.

When the snow-covered man stepped inside, she called out, "Welcome to our hearth, kind sir. Do you need a postcard?"

XVI

Saturday, January 5

Here we are at the Scenic-Vu Motel on Saturday.
Snowed in. The Big Bear Canyon was closed to traffic
yesterday at noon because of heavy snowfall. Mr. Bernelli called Mr. Flinders on the two-way radio at the
General Store and asked him to notify our parents.

Now I have been snowed in and snowed out of Bear
Flats many times (the Big Bear Canyon road being a
narrow, winding, ungraded road along the edge of Bear
River), but never in a motel with a bunch of misfits
who think weekends don't count.

Jordy and Drift won't read their novels because they
say the rules don't apply on weekends. They left early
this morning in their moon boots.

I spent the day pulling up mildewed carpet in Room
1, earning gas money to drive the misfits around. Won-

dering if Jinny Thornwall will reconsider. Knowing she won't. Totally depressed.

Just before dark they all came home, cold and wet and hungry. They looked at me and asked, "What's to eat?"

I hardly recognized the Dudettes, standing in the doorway, letting the north wind blow in. They had been up at LuDawn's Beauty Shop all day getting frizzed. They are beginning to look just like town girls.

I had no idea where the Dudes had been, but they were wet and shivering in their moon boots. They may have stood outside LuDawn's all day, watching the girls getting frizzed. I was too tired and hungry to care.

"So, what's to eat?" Drift shouted.

"Whatever it is," Helen said, "divide it with us girls and Ralphy. Just knock on our door. Anything will do."

"Hurry, though," Netty the Tall added. "We are starving and our expensive perms are getting wet."

They were all looking at me.

"I'm going to Al's Drive-In for a hamburger," I said.

"Great. We'll all go," Martin said, heading for the door.

"Let's go," Mona the Short called.

"Not until your gas tax is paid," I said pointedly. I grabbed my Levi's jacket and my keys.

There was a silence as cold as the north wind.

Then Drift said, "We don't have any money for a stupid gas tax. We just have enough for food."

"That's right," Mona said. "So if you won't let us

113

ride uptown with you, bring us all back hamburgers."

"Sorry," I said, walking out the door. "I am not responsible on Saturdays."

Sunday, January 6

As I have mentioned before, I have enough problems of my own just being Jacob R. Callahan without being Chairman of the Social Misfits.

Drift called Mrs. Matz on the telephone just before noon and said, "Help. We're starving!" Of course, she invited us all over to her house for a chicken dinner. I did not go.

Martin, the psychologist, is incapable of finding his own dirty socks to put into the paper sack inside the closet. I have to search them out by the odor and then direct him to them. He is one sloppy psychologist.

And my own little brother, I am sorry to say, is oversensitive. He still tries to act like Drift, and walks in his sleep as a result. Last night I found him walking in the snow up to Food King.

As soon as I got Jordy back into bed, a loud thumping came from Room 8. Gosh, who is missing there? I wondered. I pulled on my Levi's and dashed over.

"Call a doctor, call a doctor," Netty cried, pulling me inside. "Mona is throwing up all over. And it smells like poison. Go in there, Jake. Quick!"

So old Doctor Jake rushed into the bathroom and almost tripped over Mona leaning over the john. She looked terrible.

"Should I call Mrs. Matz?" Helen called from her bed.

"Wait," I said. "Don't wake up any more people. It may just be something she ate."

I held Mona's forehead while she threw up into the john, the way Angel does for me.

"How can you stand it?" Helen screeched. She had a pillow over her head.

"Is she poisoned?" Netty asked, peering around the door. She was holding her nose.

"Probably not," I said.

After a while Mona looked up, her face drained of color. She looked like a little wilted flower that any gust of wind could blow away. I felt terrible for not bringing her a hamburger.

"Can you help me to the bed?" she moaned.

I guided her over to her bed, fluffed the pillow, and covered her—I think with a Bethlehem Star. Then I pulled up a chair for myself.

"I guess you don't feel like a hamburger, do you?" I asked.

She moaned again.

"I didn't think so," I said, "but I just wanted you to know I would go get you one." I patted her pale little hands sticking out of the covers.

She smiled faintly.

"It's two o'clock in the morning," Netty said. "Al's Drive-In is closed."

"I would wake up old Al."

Now Mona was patting *my* hand.

"I'll go fix some medicine," I said, getting up. Over

in the kitchenette I mixed a little baking soda in a glass of warm water and took it back to her.

She sat up, and I propped two pillows behind her back.

"Sip it slowly," I said.

Meanwhile, I sat in the chair by her bed and waited—and looked around. First thing, I noticed the pictures above the beds, two pictures just alike: *Deer in Aspen* and *Deer in Aspen*.

Other than that, Mrs. Christensen, that motel room looked just like the Robbinses' home in Bear Flats—bound in leather with a scent of pine. Now what would Miss Millet, psychology teacher extraordinaire, say about that?

She would say it is natural, I suppose, because Mr. Robbins is a leatherworker who makes cowboy boots (although I didn't know he made leather bedspreads), and Mrs. Robbins makes cedar sachets.

Poor Helen. She is almost snuffed out of Room 8, except for ugly Ralphy on her bed. But together, they do make a definite statement.

After a while Mona slid down her pillow. "I thought I was dying," she whispered. "But I guess not. I feel better already. The baking soda must have helped. Thanks."

I wiped her face with a warm washcloth, and rubbed her feet to get them warm. I said I would sit by her bed for a while longer to see if she needed anything. I told Netty to clean up the bathroom.

"You're not my boss, Jake," she snapped. "You clean it up."

"You're her sister," I snapped back. "Now go clean it up."

She marched off to the bathroom.

As I said, Mrs. Christensen, I have enough problems of my own. . . .

Monday, January 7

No roast. No advice.

After school we went up to Food King to replenish our supplies. Mr. Hopkins, the manager, charged the groceries because we are regular customers and he is a nice man.

I charged the gas tax because I am either a real leisure Dude or a pushover.

I helped Jordy make tuna-fish patties for supper. I spoil him, but what the heck? I even told him I would do dishes for him if he would start reading a novel.

He and Drift debated a long time in front of Mrs. Matz's bookcase, and when they finally decided, they decided on the same book, *The African Queen*.

I told them to draw straws. Jordy drew the long one, I am happy to say, and got *The African Queen*.

Drift sulked, but settled for *Huckleberry Finn* because I told him it was similar. At least, a raft goes down a river.

I've had so much difficulty trying to enforce two rules, I'm glad I made no more. How could I enforce more?

Thursday, January 10

Spaghetti all over the kitchenette. I wonder if it makes Martin feel like a great *chef de cuisine* when it's all over the place, or if he's just sloppy.

"If we all make the honor roll and pay our gas tax," Jordy asked after supper, "can we celebrate?" He carefully placed a cold noodle in *The African Queen*.

"Sure," I said, "if you remove that noodle from Mrs. Matz's book."

"Like steaks or prime rib?" Drift asked.

"Sure. Anything we can pay for."

"I have never had prime rib," Martin confessed. "I would not even know how to cook it."

"The chef will do that," Jordy said. "We'll just eat it."

I did not comment because prime rib reminded me of Jinny Thornwall.

"The last time I had prime rib—" Drift began.

"How about prime rib at the Branding Iron?" Jordy asked.

We all agreed it sounded great.

"Let's tell the girls," Drift said. He took off his boot and pounded on the wall.

The three frizzy-haired, barefoot Beauty Queens were at our door immediately.

"Who's poisoned now?" Netty asked.

"What was all the pounding about if no one is throwing up?" Helen demanded.

"You want us to turn down a TV with a cut cord?" Mona asked.

They looked sort of cute standing framed in our

doorway in their Mickey Mouse sweatshirts. With frizzy hair and bare feet and blood-red polish on their toes!

"You are cordially invited to a Dutch treat prime rib dinner at the Branding Iron in a couple of weeks," I said, "if—"

"Don't worry about us," Mona said, tossing her frizzy head. "Look to your own house." She glanced over at our spaghetti plates on the table. "Gross," she muttered.

Thursday, January 31

Prime rib at the Branding Iron tonight, Mrs. Christensen, and not once did I think about Jinny Thornwall. These frizzy-haired Beauty Queens from Bear Flats almost take my breath away.

We sat in a big corner booth—Males on one side, Females on the other—and told jokes and sang along to country music. When we were not eating, that is.

I kept an eye on Martin when the waiters came around. You never know when he might try his chicken act on people. And I did not let Mona sit close to an electrical outlet. (I am getting paranoid like Angel.)

The girls looked about as good as girls can look. They tossed their heads a lot, which showed off their new frizzies and their earrings—tiny red hearts and golden rings. They also tapped their painted fingernails on the table a lot. And smiled.

Right in the middle of my prime rib I felt the impulse to make a toast. So I raised my fork and proclaimed, "To us!"

We all thrust our forks together above the table—some with pieces of prime rib still attached, I am sorry to say—and repeated together, "To us, the Bear Flatters!"

And yes, we had Flaming Cherries Jubilee for dessert.

Afterward, as we piled into the car, Jordy said, "Should we go over to the Gem and see old John Wayne?"

"It isn't John Wayne tonight," Martin said, nodding toward the theater marquee. "It's something new and violent."

"Besides," I added, "the Gem has sticky floors."

"Gross!" the girls all said.

"And if there is one thing Bear Flatters cannot tolerate," Martin said, "it is—"

"Sticky floors," we all said in unison.

So we cruised Main, laughing our heads off for no reason at all. Unless it was because:

1. The Christmas lights are still blinking the entire length of the Scenic-Vu;
2. All our names are on the honor roll of good old Pine Valley High School;
3. The school year is half over; and
4. We were cruising Main in an old blue Thunderbird!

As I have been writing in this journal by the bed lamp, I thought Jordy was asleep. But he just rolled over a few minutes ago and said to me, "It's nice to be on your own, isn't it, Jake?"

"Sure is," I agreed.

"Just lying here like we are camping out in a tent. Quiet enough to think. Quiet enough to hear your own self breathing. Not worrying about tomorrow because your homework is done. And no TV commercials interrupting it all."

"It is real nice, Jordy," I said.

"You're the one who makes it that way, Jake."

"Thanks, Jordy."

"Good night, Jake."

"Good night, Jordy."

He rolled back over and went to sleep. I don't think he will walk in his sleep again.

XVII

Monday, February 4

Now that Motel Management is under control, I could try Popularity at School again.

But I have been wondering if that is what I really want. I like kicking around with the Bear Flatters, *irregardless* of their provincial ways.

Monday night and hot dogs.

At the beginning of the second semester we drew for cooking days again. Would you believe, Mrs. Christensen, Drift drew Monday just as he wanted. Only Drift's mother does not cook roast beef on Sunday. Sunday is a complete day of rest for Mrs. Davis.

"You want leftover tuna-fish sandwiches?" Drift asked.

"Hot dogs will have to do," I said, "but no potato chips. Buy potato salad or cottage cheese."

"Remember junk food?" Martin said. "At the beginning of school?"

"No," Drift said, "I can't remember it."

"Remember all those potato chips in the carpet and pop cans in the bathtub?" Martin continued.

"Popcorn on top of the beds, popcorn in the beds . . ." Jordy added.

"We were real pigs," Martin said.

"Pigs no more," Drift said. "Guess what's for dessert." He opened the refrigerator and carefully lifted out a bowl.

"I followed a lady who bought raisins and Jell-O!" he said.

Monday, February 11

Big announcement at school today by Mr. Van Wagoner: Science Fair. Begin projects today and display them in April.

Martin and I are going to make bridges and enter them in the bridge-building contest. We can buy balsawood kits with instructions from Mr. Van Wagoner. Most of the boys in the school are making bridges.

Drift says he is going to make the solar system. And Jordy a volcano.

Wednesday, February 13

"How big a volcano?" Mrs. Matz asked when she heard the big announcement.

123

Jordy spread out his arms. "As big as I can make it."

"And what about the solar system?" she asked.

"Oh, it can just hang from a ceiling," Drift said, looking up.

"Remember, we have to transport the projects to school," I cautioned.

"The gym has a wonderful ceiling," Drift said, grinning. "And the custodian will have an extension ladder."

"Two bridges, one volcano, and one solar system," Mrs. Matz said. "What about the girls?"

The Dudettes said because the projects are optional, they are not participating. They would rather spend their free time quilting.

Mrs. Matz was pleased as punch to hear that.

"Normal and right," she said. "If the men would build the bridges and the women stitch the quilts, we would have fewer problems in this world."

I suggested she write the president.

Thursday, February 14

Now building bridges is more like it, Mrs. C. This is not saying anything against the beloved language with its beautiful metaphors. It is just saying that Jake R. Callahan likes to build bridges.

By the way, Happy Valentine's Day.

Tuesday, February 19

Mrs. Matz was happy to find out that our science projects are all quiet endeavors—no electric saws or jackhammers needed.

Building a bridge requires only sharp knives and Elmer's glue. And megapatience. The object is to make the strongest bridge possible with the lightweight wood and cardboard provided in the kit.

Every night Martin and I work on our bridges in Laboratory 1, formerly called Room 1.

Jordy is bulding his volcano out of modeling clay, a different color for each layer of rock in the earth: black igneous, gray metamorphic, pink sedimentary, and a moss-green cone.

It's going to be a work of art.

So far Drift has Mercury, Venus, and Earth in papier-mâché hanging from the ceiling. They are all made to scale and positioned around the light fixture, which for now represents the sun.

We are all living geniuses.

Thursday, March 7

For weeks we Dudes have secluded ourselves in Laboratory 1 every night, dedicating ourselves to science. Tonight we reluctantly allowed the Dudettes and Mrs. Matz in for a preview, because they said they could contain their curiosity no longer.

At first they were not overly impressed with the

two fragile-looking bridges that Martin and I are making. Until we started piling on the *World Book*s.

"These intricately constructed bridges will hold up hundreds of pounds," I explained, "but we won't find out how much until the science fair. All the bridges break, even the winner's."

"Gross," Mona said.

Jordy's volcano was finished down to the tin can inside the cone, and he was anxious to demonstrate. When he had the attention of everyone, he pulled a small paper sack out of his pocket.

"Ammonium dichromate crystals and match heads," he said, pouring part of it inside the cone. Then he lit a match and dropped it into the cone.

Wow! Talk about Mount Vesuvius, Mrs. Christensen. You should have seen those flames. And the dark-green ash rolling down the cone and over the table and falling to the floor.

"All right!" the girls cried. They rushed to open the door.

"Come back, come back," Drift called, not to be outdone by Jordy. "You haven't seen science yet."

They came back and sat on the floor as far from the green ash as possible.

Poor Mrs. Matz was still standing in her original place. Stunned, you could say.

"Are you ready?" Drift shouted. He lifted the end of an extension cord that ran up the wall and across the ceiling to a magnificent sun, a chicken-wire sun covered with yellow cellophane paper with a light bulb inside.

"Ready for what?" Mrs. Matz asked weakly.

"The sun! It lights up the entire solar system."

"Ready," the girls called.

Drift plugged in the cord. Wow! We were in total darkness.

"An eclipse," Drift gasped. "Did I do that?"

"Oh, my soul," Mrs. Matz shrieked. "You have blown a fuse."

The entire motel was dark. Doors flew open and guests called, "What's going on here? Where are the lights?"

"So sorry, so sorry," Mrs. Matz called, running up and down the sidewalk. "Someone must have blown a fuse. Where's a flashlight? Oh, where is a flashlight?"

I ran to my car for a flashlight and told Mrs. Matz to direct me to the fuse box.

It was an old thing in a closet in the office, but I finally figured it out. But no fuses.

"I think there are some over in my house," Mrs. Matz exclaimed. "I'll run and get them, Jake. Oh, Carter, my dear, why didn't we buy a Laundromat?"

I held the flashlight at the office door while Mrs. Matz raced over to her house, moaning and waving her arms. The unhappy guests were still complaining.

"Let's check out of here, Jay. First that horrid smell and now no lights. We could be dead by morning and not even know it."

"Of course. I saw another motel—the City Motel, I think it was called."

"It's the Uptown," Jordy interrupted. "And you won't like it."

"Why not?"

"For one thing it really isn't uptown. Mr. Angus Webb just thinks it is uptown."

"Well?"

"And another thing. No hot plates."

The man coughed. "No hot plates, you say?"

"But the most important thing," Mona called. "No view."

"No view?"

"That's right. No view."

Mrs. Matz had found a fuse by then, and we hurried back into the office. I replaced the fuse, and the lights came on again. Mrs. Matz collapsed on the sofa.

Drift rushed in, swinging a pair of pliers.

"So sorry, Mrs. Matz," he said. "But don't worry about a thing. There was no damage to the solar system. Part of the chicken-wire sun must have touched the light-bulb wires inside. It's fixed now."

"Just the chicken-wire sun touching the light-bulb wires," Mrs. Matz wailed. "Oh, Carter, my dear. Was it you who said, 'Not a Laundromat'?"

XVIII

Tuesday, March 12

Did I say that Motel Management was under control? If so, Mrs. Christensen, it was an overstatement—a hyperbole, I believe you call it.

Last night about twelve o'clock I woke up to the sound of tapping on the window. I shot straight up in bed, wondering who liked me now.

The tapping continued. I slid out of bed and moved cautiously over to the window. Someone was there, all right.

"Hey, Mona. Hey, Mona, babes."

I dashed to the door and opened it a crack. "You have the wrong window, dude," I hissed. "Get out and don't ever come back to this motel."

That boy took off "like a streak of lightning," as my dad would say. I did not chase after him because I do not like running barefoot through the snow. I just hoped I scared the liver out of him.

I felt the incident warranted a meeting. This morning, halfway to school on Elm Street, I stopped the car.

"I am calling a meeting now," I said.

"Now?" Mona shouted from the backseat. "On the way to school?"

"In the car?" Jordy exclaimed.

"The car is the only private place," I said. "If Mrs. Matz hears about this, she will definitely throw us out on our heads."

"What's this meeting on Elm Street about?" Martin asked. He reached his long arms over everybody and locked both doors.

"The same old rules," I said.

"The same old rules—Study Hard and Have Fun?" Netty asked.

"Oh, sure," Drift drawled. "Study Hard and Have Fun. I've been trying to remember those two. They have become so much a part of me that I'd almost forgotten them. Study Hard and Have Fun."

"Shut up, Drift," Martin said.

"Just one more comment," Drift said. "If there is any time left after the meeting, I would like to solicit donations for a worthy cause—"

"Shut up, Drift!" Martin said again.

"This meeting," I said, "is to inform you that if anyone sneaks out of the motel during the night, he is breaking the rules. He may think it is fun, but the consequences will not be. Any questions?"

130

"Is this a hypothetical situation?" Helen demanded from the back.

"You can say this is a hypothetical situation. And against the rules." I started the car.

"That would be a lot of fun—sneaking out of a motel," Drift said.

Jordy leaned over to Drift. "Where would we go if we did?" (Good old Jordy.)

"Oh, up on Hiller's Hill, Ten Acres picnic area, the rodeo bleachers. I could name a dozen or more places," Drift whispered loudly.

"Does this warning refer to sleepwalking?" Jordy asked.

"No, Jordy," I said.

I revved the engine. "Any more questions?"

"Did you say *he* back there?" Martin asked. "I don't think this subject applies to the Males."

"It does not apply to the Females, either," Mona snapped. She flashed daggers at me through the rear-view mirror.

"Good," I said. "Meeting adjourned."

Thursday, March 14

The very next night after the meeting, Mrs. Christensen, the very next night. *Irregardless* of the warning.

I do not understand girls.

Shortly after midnight I woke up and sat up in bed.

Sure enough, someone was tapping on the window. Only this time on the window of Room 8.

I pulled on my clothes, trying to formulate a plan at the same time. Something effective this time.

Peering behind the draperies I saw Mona come out, giggling, and join the dude. They walked across the parking lot and turned east on Main.

I grabbed an old parka and ran out to my car. I followed them, with the lights off, past the farm-implement yard and up to Steve's Garage. There they got into the dude's pickup truck.

It wasn't hard to follow the pickup. When he turned north, I knew where he was headed. It was the road to Mrs. Whitely's house that I had run up and down a thousand times last year. I could drive it without lights anytime.

He pulled off the road at Ten Acres picnic area, stopped the pickup, and turned off the lights. I pulled in behind him and turned my lights on bright. Now I call that effective. I only wish I had been in the cab to see the reaction.

I grabbed a flashlight and sauntered over to the dude's window and flashed the light in his face.

"Open up," I called, tapping on his window.

He rolled down the window. "Officer—" he whined.

"I'm no officer."

"It's Jake!" Mona exclaimed. "What are you doing here?"

"What are you doing here?" I repeated.

"It is none of your business what I'm doing, so go home and leave us alone."

Now that I could see the dude, I could see he was

big Budd Swaney. Real big. I wanted to go home just as Mona said.

"I'm here to take you home, Ramona Lisa," I said.

"We're just having a little fun," Budd said. "Now beat it. And get that light out of my face before I smash it in yours."

I flashed the light down to the seat, lighting up a six-pack of beer.

"Get out, Mona," I said. "And get in my car. This dude does not like you as a person. He likes you because you live in a motel. It's the motel he likes, not you."

Big Budd opened the pickup door. "Wanna fight about it?"

I said sure because what else could I say? All the experience I have had with girls—

He knocked me down, and I held on to his Levi's jacket and pulled him down on top of me. We rolled around a while on the frozen ground, getting scratched up.

When we let go of each other, we almost lost each other in the dark. But we started in again, over patches of snow, frozen mud, and broken tree limbs. I tasted blood in my mouth, and I wanted to throw up.

Mona screamed from the pickup for us to stop, but we didn't. We were fighting in earnest.

"I'm going for the sheriff if you don't stop," Mona yelled. She started the truck.

Budd jumped up at that and rushed over to his pickup.

"Get out!" he yelled at Mona. "You're too much trouble."

He jumped in his truck, maneuvered it between my car and a picnic table, and roared away.

It was quiet after that, and I thought perhaps Mona had gone with him. I dragged myself over to a picnic table, crawled up, and leaned over on the table. And moaned.

"You big idiot," Mona said from the other side of the table. "You great big idiot. We were just having fun. Can't you allow anyone to have fun?"

I was bleeding and she didn't even care.

"Burning down the motel was one thing, Ramona Lisa Robbins," I shouted. "But this! This is something else—in another category—something that would be of vital interest to the board of education.

"If Budd Swaney tells one person—just one—the board of education will come knocking at the Scenic-Vu before the week is over."

I banged my fist on the picnic table. "This does not affect you alone, Ramona Lisa. The future of all the Bear Flatters is at stake. Think about it. Think about what you have done."

"All you care about are those two rules of yours," she snapped.

"Those two rules of ours," I said, "protect us from the madhouse. Let's get going."

She hurried over to the car and climbed in the back-seat. I got in the front and reached for the keys.

No keys.

I felt in my pockets, then down on the floor.

"What's the matter?" Mona asked.

"I've lost the keys," I said. "Help me look for them."

We felt all around the car, and all around where the

134

pickup had been parked. We crawled all around the picnic table.

I stumbled onto the flashlight, and using it, we went back over every inch of ground we had already covered.

"Sleep on, Mrs. Matz. Sleep on," I muttered.

Mona began crying. "Should we start walking? I'm so cold I can't stay here much longer."

"No," I said. "They have to be here somewhere. We'll find them."

"What did you do with them, Jake?" Mona cried in exasperation.

"I put them in my pocket," I snarled, "but they must have fallen out when I was fighting for my life with your big ape friend. He bit me, you know. The big ape."

"Check your pockets again," Mona said.

"I have. A dozen times."

After a while I gave up and went back to the car. My head was throbbing and my back hurt.

"We are about halfway between Mrs. Whitely's and town," I said. "Let's rest a few minutes and then start walking to town."

"Don't you have a blanket in this car?" Mona asked.

"Locked in the trunk."

I leaned back against the seat, trying to rest my aching body. At the same time, something jabbed me in the back. I reached around. Keys in the back of my parka?

I felt in my pockets again—and found a hole in the lining of one. I breathed a deep sigh of relief.

"What now?" Mona asked from the backseat.

"Nothing," I said. "But I guess I'll have another look before we start walking." I opened the door.

"Should I come?" Mona asked, her teeth chattering.

"Suit yourself."

Mona crawled around the car again on her hands and knees, and I went over to a tree and leaned against it. I dropped the keys and stepped on them.

"What luck," I called, stooping down to pick up the keys. "I found them, Mona."

"Oh, Jake," she cried. "Thank goodness. Quick, start the car. Turn on the heater. Drive fast."

On the way back to town I gave her the good old purpose-of-life talk. I told her not to get discouraged here in Pineville, Idaho, which was only step two on the ladder of life.

I explained about the view from the motel and the view from the top of the ladder. I reminded her about her dad working hard on cowboy boots and her mother on those cedar needle sachets so they could pay her way up the ladder.

Now that I think about it, I was really an overbearing slob. I guess I thought she was my little sister.

Anyway, when we pulled up at the Scenic-Vu, she got out and slammed the door hard enough to wake up the whole world, Mrs. Matz in particular.

And she said, "Shut up, you overbearing slob!"

XIX

Friday, March 15

I stayed here to work this weekend. Also I did not want to explain my swollen face to Angel. It was hard enough explaining it to the Bear Flatters.

"You didn't look like that when you went to bed," Jordy said.

"I had a nightmare," I said.

I did not go to school today. I went up to the clinic and had a couple of stitches in my chin and a tetanus shot for the bite on my shoulder.

Jordy went with me, and I told him the whole story, except the part about the keys in my parka lining.

"He bit me, Jordy. The big ape bit me," I kept saying.

"Next time wake me up," he scolded. "I'll go with you." (Good old Jordy.)

When we came out of Dr. Lee's office, Mona was waiting in the reception room. Her face was blotched and puffy. She looked worse than I did.

"I didn't know you were hurt, Jake," she said. "I couldn't see in the dark. I am so sorry. I hope you can forget last night."

I said, "I can forget anything, Ramona Lisa. Last night, the night before that, the night you were poisoned—"

"Don't be sarcastic!" she snapped. "I was trying to apologize." She stomped on ahead to the car.

Jordy and I walked outside into the bracing cold air. Good old Idaho air. I took a deep breath to clear my head.

At the car, I opened the door for Mona. "I accept your apology, Ramona Lisa," I said.

"Oh, forget it." She jumped into the car and glared at me. "And don't call me Ramona Lisa."

I have been calling her Ramona Lisa since she was born. She is really "up on a high horse," as my dad would say.

Monday, March 18

After school I went to the motel office to help the girls with math as usual.

Mrs. Matz said, "Netty and Helen, will you do me a favor? Run back to my house and see if you can find a spool of purple quilting thread in my machine drawers. Look hard."

That left Mona and me alone with her.

"Horace Leander from the board was here today," she said. She did not look up from quilting.

We both froze on the spot.

"What did he want?" I asked.

"I'm not sure," she said. "Maybe the Uptown has turned in an application for next year. Just in case, I told him I was planning on the same situation next year.

"I did most of the talking, I'm afraid. For one thing, I told him that you kids have more effective meetings than the board of education has."

"Thanks, Mrs. Matz," I said. "Thanks very much."

She began stitching faster. "I also told him to consider the source. I asked him if Budd Swaney is on the Pine Valley High School honor roll. I told him if he is, report to the board. If he isn't, consider the source."

Mona threw her arms around Mrs. Matz, almost choking her.

"Watch out. I'll stick myself with this needle and ruin the quilt," she said, laughing.

"I better go check the bulletin board," I said.

I jumped into my car and drove over to school at full speed. I dashed up the steps and around the corner to Mr. Fitzhugh's office.

Horace Leander was standing like a bulldozer in front of the bulletin board, reading names aloud and writing them down in a little notebook.

I stood next to him and read the list up and down,

and down and up. There was no Budd Swaney on the honor roll.

"Consider the source," I said pointedly to Mr. Leander. "Consider the source."

I walked out slightly above ground level, got into my old blue car, and drove back to the Scenic-Vu.

XX

Wednesday, March 20

This morning at the crack of dawn I pulled the quilts off Drift and told him that it was the first day of spring.

"So what?" he growled.

"I read in the paper yesterday that if a person washes his face in the first dew of spring and then walks backward into the house, his freckles will disappear."

Drift's chubby face lit up like a Christmas tree. "What about a motel?"

"Same thing." My conscience was beginning to prick.

"How many steps?"

"It didn't say. Just keep walking backward until you are inside."

Drift nodded. "I'll make sure I don't do that," he said. "Nobody is taking anything from me—especially my freckles."

He slid back under the quilts.

As I've said before, Mrs. Christensen, Drift is a real pro.

Monday, April 8

I have spring fever, Mrs. Christensen. Would you believe I asked Ramona Lisa to the Senior Prom this coming Friday?

I asked her while driving home to Bear Flats last Wednesday for spring vacation. The other Bear Flatters were pulling faces at us from the back window of the school bus, which did not contribute any romance to the occasion.

After saying yes to the dance, Ramona Lisa said she has liked me ever since I was six years old.

I said she certainly has had a funny way of showing it.

She said I don't know very much about girls.

I agreed to that.

About that time Mr. Bernelli honked his horn at Drift's shrine, which is still just an X on a quaking aspen at the side of the road. Mona and I kept a moment's silence out of habit.

I said to Mona maybe we could build a shrine of our own on this road, at the spot where I asked her for our first date. As I said, Mrs. C., I have spring fever. Please feel free to edit.

I had wanted to pull up in Bear Flats the first time in my car with all the Bear Flatters in tow, smiling and waving. Sort of like a homecoming float. But Mr.

142

Bernelli said he was required under contract to the board of education to drive the bus, and someone had better be on it.

Anyway, as each Bear Flatter got off the bus at his stop, he came back and climbed in with Mona and me. Then we pulled up in front of my house and honked.

It takes Angel and Dad a while to adjust to change. Angel did a lot of looking and Dad drove *me* around. But by Sunday they had both consented to ride to church with the top down and me driving. They looked like two juvenile judges all the way to church, but as they stepped out, Dad turned to Angel and said, "Now that's what I call initiative."

Angel nodded. "If you say so, George. If you say so."

Back at the motel—

My first impression when I stopped in at the office this morning was that Mrs. Matz had been robbed. Without a quilt spread across it, the room looked like a typical bleak motel office—Naugahyde sofa and TV.

It was nice to see the postcards again, however.

Would you believe Mrs. Matz finished eight quilts this winter, with some help from the girls? Eight queen-size quilts: one Motel Special, one Irish Chain, one Shoo-fly, one Bear Paw, one Log Cabin, two Faded Denims from all the old Levi's in Bear Flats, and one purple-and-white Bow Tie.

Mona suggested that she sell them at the boutique in Pocatello, where her mother sells the cedar needle sachets. Mrs. Matz is going to talk to Mrs. Robbins about it.

But, she says, they are not all for sale. Guess who is getting the purple-and-white Bow Tie for graduation?

Spring fever or not, Mrs. C., I have been working on my model bridge almost every night for a month. I have just a few more cross supports to glue on. Even now it holds up A through F of Mrs. Matz's *World Books*.

Martin is finished—but he is definitely a genius. Jordy's volcano has been finished for weeks, and he practices the explosion whenever he can afford more chemicals. The floor of Laboratory 1 is almost completely coated with dark-green ash.

Drift's solar system is finished, too, and it makes a spectacular sight hanging from the ceiling. He keeps taking down the sun, however, trying to mold it into a perfect sphere.

It is possible that Drift will become the first smart aleck in space.

Spring fever again. At midnight we Dudes thumped on the Dudettes' wall and took them for a cruise around town with the top down. The air smelled great.

I'll bet there is no air in the entire U.S.A. like Idaho air. Maybe in the whole world.

Wednesday, April 10

This afternoon I drove up to the Rosebud and ordered a rosebud corsage for Mona for Friday night.

144

The place was filled with dudes ordering rosebuds. I started talking to Joe Grant, and he said he would like to double with me Friday. I said fine, I would take my car.

He said good, he only has a pickup. He invited Mona and me to his girlfriend's house for dinner before the dance, and then to his house afterward for a John Wayne movie on the VCR. I said fine again.

Mrs. Matz was waving frantically from the office steps when I drove up to the motel.

"Call a meeting, Jake," she exclaimed. "Call a meeting."

The Bear Flatters were already sitting in their usual places in the office when I walked in, so I said, "Meeting called."

It seems that the good reputation of the Bear Flatters has filtered through the town of Pineville. Horace Leander had been to see Mrs. Matz with the news that two separate parties had made application to the board of education for our room and board next school year. Both parties said they could offer a better environment than a permissive motel.

The board of education was thinking of separating the girls and the boys between the two couples.

"What did you say?" I asked.

"Hogwash is what I said," Mrs. Matz replied. "Then I said it again. I was so upset, I'm afraid I was not very effective." She clutched her head.

"She did show him the science laboratory," Martin said. "Who else in this town could provide a separate room for science projects?"

"No one," I said.

"And who else would forgo TV to chaperon tutorage every night of the school year?

"Who else would provide quilting lessons for the girls and a fully equipped garage for the boys?

"And part-time work?"

"No one," I repeated.

"I could not think of any of those things, I was so upset," Mrs. Matz said. "And they are going to decide at their next board meeting, on the twenty-fourth of this month. Oh, woe is me."

"Don't worry, Mrs. Matz," I said. "We will all be here next year. All except me, that is. And I now nominate Martin Rawley to take my position as— What is my position?"

"Keeper of the Two Sacred Rules?" Drift suggested.

"*Irregardless*, all in favor say aye."

"Aye."

"And don't worry. My dad will attend that board of education meeting, and probably Angel, too."

"Our folks will go, too," Mona said, "if we ask them."

"Mine, too," Helen said.

Martin and Drift said the same.

"My dad can make headlines all by himself," I said. "But I'll tell him. Meeting adjourned."

We went to our rooms. And to celebrate life in Room 9, we cooked New York steaks for supper.

XXI

Saturday, April 13

The Senior Prom was great. The dinner was great and the party after was great. The weather was great.

Mona looked great. She wore a pink taffeta dress with puffed sleeves that looked like two big pink roses. She made it herself on Mrs. Matz's sewing machine—with a lot of help from good old Mrs. Matz, I imagine. She calls it Ashes of Roses.

Afterward, in the car in the Scenic-Vu parking lot, right under the old moon, I held Mona's hand, admiring her in that pink-rose dress. Occasionally I caught the faint scent of rosebuds from the corsage on her wrist.

Mona had a dreamy look in her eyes, and a little smile played on her lips.

"Are you thinking of John Wayne?" I asked.

She looked at me, surprised. "Not exactly. Not John Wayne."

"Who then?"

"Jake Callahan."

My heart nearly leaped out of the convertible.

"What a coincidence," I said. "I was thinking of you, too. How beautiful you look in that pink dress with the roses on the sleeves." I touched the folds of taffeta on her shoulders.

"Thanks."

"How much fun you were tonight. How much fun you always are—and sincere—"

"And intelligent and witty," Mona added.

"Not to mention audacious and egotistical—"

"Chic and flamboyant—"

"Supercilious—"

(We came up with some good adjectives, Mrs. C.)

"Mona," I said, trying to prolong the evening, "do you want to trade one of your *Deer in Aspen* for one of our *Fisherman with Trout*? That is, if we can pry them off the walls?"

A simple question like that makes a girl cry?

Between tears she said, "I don't want to go to school next year without you, Jake. And you won't even be home on weekends."

"Some weekends," I said. "And holidays will be great."

"I write good letters," she said, dabbing at her eyes.

"Love letters?"

She nodded.

I could have sat there forever, holding her hand, gazing at her. Mona Robbins—a precious thing of beauty with the most beautiful name I had ever heard. Mona, Mona, Ramona Lisa.

As I said, I could have sat there forever, but Jordy

148

popped up out of nowhere and leaned over the door. He had stayed over for the weekend to chaperon for Angel, I suspect.

"Do you know what time it is?" he scolded. "I'm sleepy!" (Good old Jordy.)

Monday, April 22

Big night at Pine Valley High School. Science fair in the gym.

Two professors came from the university to act as judges, bringing with them a small hydraulic press for testing the strength of the model bridges.

Dozens of bridges were lined up on the cafeteria tables, some collapsing before the judges even reached their table.

At least mine did not do that. It held up 592 pounds before it cracked.

Would you believe, Mrs. Christensen, that Martin's held up 678 pounds? He took first place. He received a big certificate and a check for two hundred dollars. And his cracked bridge will be immortalized in the school trophy case.

That's what he gets for keeping his hat on, he said.

The other projects were judged earlier in the day, and Jordy and Drift both received blue ribbons. Not bad, I'd say.

After the bridge contest tonight, everyone milled around the gymnasium observing the original projects. Volcanoes were blowing and engines were humming. It was great.

149

Drift's solar system was the only project hanging from the ceiling, and I must admit it looked impressive. Mr. Fitzhugh and his wife spent a lot of time standing under it, looking up.

Toward the middle of the evening, I saw Mr. Fitzhugh point to the long line of extension cords that stretched from the sun, across the ceiling, and down the wall to an outlet. And then dangled.

It was just too tempting for a principal to resist, I guess. He plugged in the cord.

The entire gymnasium went black. Oh, madness!

That took care of this year's science fair.

Tuesday, April 23

The school year is winding down, as you say, Mrs. Christensen. My arm is also winding down. And it is perfectly hunky-dory with me if you call for these journals on May 1, three weeks before school closes.

But—describe myself again? I did that last September. And I am just the same old Jacob R. Callahan in April. I cook great hamburgers on Thursdays. Last semester I cooked great hamburgers on Wednesdays.

I am still tall and thin and possibly the fastest runner in school. Everyone knows that.

And I still cannot roll my tongue. I could practice until the cows come home and still I could not roll my tongue. But who cares?

I still think about a Ford pickup truck because I am still living in the Pickup Capital of the World. I won't be living here much longer, however, and I really like my old blue Thunderbird. All paid for by myself.

One of these years I might turn in my old blue car for a pickup truck and come back here and cruise Main with Mona in the cab beside me and all the Bear Flatters I can find piled in the back.

I still think about girls, mostly beautiful, genuine girls from Bear Flats. Mostly Mona Robbins.

But what I think about most of all is graduating from Pine Valley High School with at least a 3.5 GPA and going to the University of Idaho next year. I'm anxious to see the view from step three.

My biggest worry is about the Bear Flatters living away from home next year—without me. But with Martin as the Keeper of the Two Sacred Rules, and Mrs. Matz as chaperon, I guess they can get along without old Indispensable Me.

Occasionally I think about building a shrine on Highway 30, an expensive marble one that reads: KEEP IDAHO SCENIC FOR JACOB R. CALLAHAN.

Or: JAKE SENDS HIS LOVE.

Or: ROLL YOUR TONGUE FOR JAKE.

Or something like that. On second thought, maybe I will just donate to Drift's.

Thursday, April 25

Last night my dad and several other fathers from Bear Flats came down to Pineville for the board of education meeting. Dad spoke for all. He stood up, waved his arms, and shouted, "We are here to give you the straight poop!"

(Do you think he means "the straight scoop"?)

As I said earlier, Mrs. C., the Bear Flatters will definitely be at the Scenic-Vu Motel next year.

Dad says most of Bear Flats will be coming down on June 7 for graduation night. He has reserved all nine rooms at the Scenic-Vu, including Room 1.

Mrs. Matz is planning to turn on the No Vacancy sign *irregardless*—

Wednesday, May 1

Well, Mrs. Christensen, I don't know if this is what you wanted or not. You said last September not to make it sound like a weather report. I don't think you will be disappointed there.

I am no William Shakespeare when it comes to the beloved language, Mrs. Christensen. And I am not too original with metaphors, as you have already found out. I borrow. But I give credit.

What you have read here is, in my dad's language— but by now you already know that.

Graduate me, Mrs. Christensen. Please graduate me!

Jake

Jacob R. Callahan
Senior
Pine Valley High School
Pineville, Idaho

Addendum 1

Friday, June 7

At the Pine Valley High School Commencement Exercises this evening, Jacob R. Callahan was presented the PVHS Award of Excellence by the school principal, Marcus B. Fitzhugh, for his outstanding senior English journal.

This coveted prize consists of a one-year tuition scholarship to the University of Idaho.

On presentation of the award, the surprised but pleased recipient was lauded with a standing ovation by the students, faculty, and patrons of the high school.

Caroline A. Christensen

Mrs. Caroline A. Christensen
English Department
Pine Valley High School
Pineville, Idaho

Addendum 2

Bear Flatters of the world—
Keep your boots on!

JRC